The door oper
there in nothir
made her eyes

Her hair was wet and hung in strands around her face. Soft, silky skin dotted with cream peeped around the towel. Sleepy eyes stared back at him. Raw, primitive and all-male emotions roused his lower abdomen and below.

Wyatt handed her the case. "Here are your things. Your wallet is in the safe at the office. Just thought I'd remove temptation."

Frowning, Peyton held the towel with one hand while taking the case with the other. Her fingers brushed across his and he felt as if he'd been baptized by fire. Baptized like a teenager who had just been touched by an attractive, sexy woman for the first time.

Dear Reader,

One day my husband and I were returning home and we passed a red convertible sports car pulled over to the side of the road by a highway patrolman. A young blonde was driving, her Hollywood-style sunglasses perched on top of her head. The patrolman's arm rested on top of the windshield as he leaned in, talking to her. He was smiling. A big this-is-my-lucky-day smile. I told my husband that woman would not be getting a ticket.

From this a story began to emerge about a hard-nosed sheriff, Wyatt Carson, and a feisty socialite, Peyton Ross, who's never taken responsibility for anything in her life. Not only is Peyton caught speeding, but she offers the sheriff a bribe to let her go. Wyatt is determined to make Peyton pay for her crimes, but she is just as determined to make the high and mighty sheriff regret the day he ever put her in handcuffs.

A small warning—you probably won't like Peyton when you first meet her, but give her a chance. I promise by the end of the book you will love her. So come along and see who's the first to bend, the first to have a change of attitude, a change of heart.

I had fun writing this story, and I hope you have as much fun reading it.

With love and thanks,

Linda Warren

P.S. Make my day and let me know (good or bad) what you think of this book. You can e-mail me at Lw1508@aol.com or write me at P.O. Box 5182, Bryan, TX 77805 or visit my Web site at www.lindawarren.net or www.myspace.com/authorlindawarren. Your letters will be answered.

The Sheriff of Horseshoe, Texas

LINDA WARREN

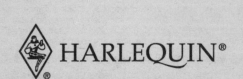

HARLEQUIN®

TORONTO • NEW YORK • LONDON
AMSTERDAM • PARIS • SYDNEY • HAMBURG
STOCKHOLM • ATHENS • TOKYO • MILAN • MADRID
PRAGUE • WARSAW • BUDAPEST • AUCKLAND

Recycling programs
for this product may
not exist in your area.

ISBN-13: 978-0-373-75253-9
ISBN-10:   0-373-75253-9

THE SHERIFF OF HORSESHOE, TEXAS

Copyright © 2009 by Linda Warren.

This edition published by arrangement with Harlequin Books S.A.

® and TM are trademarks of the publisher. Trademarks indicated with ® are registered in the United States Patent and Trademark Office, the Canadian Trade Marks Office and in other countries.

www.eHarlequin.com

Printed in U.S.A.

ABOUT THE AUTHOR

Award-winning, bestselling author Linda Warren has written twenty-one books for Harlequin Superromance and Harlequin American Romance. She grew up in the farming and ranching community of Smetana, Texas, the only girl in a family of boys. She loves to write about Texas, and from time to time scenes and characters from her childhood show up in her books. Linda lives in College Station, Texas, not far from her birthplace, with her husband, Billy, and a menagerie of wild animals, from Canada geese to bobcats. Visit her Web site at www.lindawarren.net.

Books by Linda Warren

HARLEQUIN AMERICAN ROMANCE

1042—THE CHRISTMAS CRADLE
1089—CHRISTMAS, TEXAS STYLE
        "Merry Texmas"
1102—THE COWBOY'S RETURN
1151—ONCE A COWBOY
1226—TEXAS HEIR

HARLEQUIN SUPERROMANCE

1125—THE WRONG WOMAN
1167—A BABY BY CHRISTMAS
1221—THE RIGHT WOMAN
1250—FORGOTTEN SON
1314—ALL ROADS LEAD TO TEXAS
1354—SON OF TEXAS
1375—THE BAD SON
1440—ADOPTED SON
1470—TEXAS BLUFF
1499—ALWAYS A MOTHER

ACKNOWLEDGMENTS

A big thank-you to Beverly Straub
for graciously answering my many questions
about fashion and socialites.

And a special thanks to Margie Lawson
and her Deep Editing Techniques. I thoroughly
enjoyed her workshop and getting to know her.
Thank you, Margie, for opening my eyes to the
power of words, the power of writing.

Thanks to Dorothy Kissman and Phyllis Fletcher
for once again kindly sharing information
about their hometown, Austin, Texas.

DEDICATION

I dedicate this book to the community
of Smetana, Texas, where I grew up and learned
about small-town America and bonds and
friendships that last a lifetime.

Chapter One

Sunday afternoons were made for love.

The scent of lilacs, the taste of strawberry wine and Lori. Sweet Lorelei.

His wife.

A smile tugged at Sheriff Wyatt Carson's mouth. But a second later his daydream was hijacked by the present, and gut-wrenching reality.

Painful memories sliced into his heart. When they were teenagers, Lori would call and say, "It's Sunday afternoon. Where are you?" It had been the same in college. "It's Sunday. I'll meet you in an hour." When they both had gone into law enforcement and worked a beat in Austin, those afternoons had been their special time.

But no more.

His Lori died six years ago.

The weight on his chest pressed down, feeling heavier than a two-thousand-pound bull. No air. No breath. Just pain.

At last he inhaled and he welcomed the rush of air. Yet he cursed it, too. He needed the memories. They kept him going. They kept him strong. Though years had passed, Wyatt still took life one day at a time, but the pain never lessened. It only grew deeper.

Blinking against the bright June sun, he slipped on his sunglasses and strolled to his patrol car at the courthouse. Now his Sunday afternoons were made for fishing—with his eight-year-old daughter, Jody. He'd moved from Austin to his small hometown to raise their child alone, in a safe environment. The way Lori would have wanted.

With a sigh, Wyatt slid into his car. His daughter was waiting.

Backing out, he waved at Delmar Ferguson, who owned the auto-parts store. Delmar was opening up for the afternoon trade.

Horseshoe, Texas, was much the same as it had been when Wyatt was a kid. An old two-story limestone courthouse, yellowing and graying in spots from age, sat in the center of a town square that happened to be in the shape of a horseshoe. Gnarled oaks and blooming red crepe myrtles gave the old structure a touch of beauty.

The weathered brick and mortar storefronts that surrounded the square were still the same, too. Some had been boarded up—the old furniture store, the fabric shop and the Perry Brothers' Five and Dime. The casualties of a changing America.

But new businesses had opened, including Miss Hattie's Tea Room, Flo's Antiques, Betty Jo's Candle Shop and a dollar store. The old Wiznowski family bakery was still on the corner. For five generations it had kept going strong, and probably would for years to come.

Horseshoe was the epitome of small-town America, its citizens upholding strong family values. It was a place where friendly neighbors helped each other. That had been the main reason Wyatt had chosen to come home—to heal while finding a way to live again.

For Jody.

He had to hurry because his daughter was not patient. First he had to go to the bait stand on the highway. As he reached

Texas Highway 77, which ran on the outskirts of Horseshoe, a red convertible sports car zoomed by, barely missing Mrs. Harriet Peabody as she crossed the highway from her son's fruit-and-vegetable stand.

Harriet shook her walking cane at the car in vain. Then she saw Wyatt and pointed with her cane in the direction the car had gone.

Wyatt tipped his hat, signaling that he had seen the whole thing. He turned on his siren and roared after the speeder. The first thing he noticed was the blond hair whipping in the wind. The next thing was the woman's failure to respond to the siren. She kept going—*faster.*

He clocked her going eighty-five in a seventy; through the business area the limit was fifty-five. This lady was in a big hurry. Wyatt stayed on her tail and she still made no move to stop as the siren wailed through the lazy afternoon.

Texas 77 was only two lanes, so he couldn't go around her because cars were coming from the other direction. They were about to reach the county line, so he picked up his radio to alert the highway patrol. Someone had to stop the woman before she caused an accident.

Just then an eighteen-wheeler appeared ahead of them and she had to slow down. Wyatt put down the radio as he waited for oncoming traffic to pass, and then darted into the left lane before she could. He motioned for her to pull over.

Behind her large sunglasses, he couldn't see her eyes, but her pink lips formed an angry pout. Again, she made no effort to stop. He motioned again, this time more forcefully, and he wondered if she was on drugs and not comprehending what was going on around her. No one was that arrogant or stupid to openly defy an officer of the law.

The driver of the eighteen-wheeler slowed to a crawl and the woman finally pulled onto the grassy verge, as did the big truck. Wyatt was relieved. She was boxed in and couldn't speed away once he stepped out of his car.

He turned off the siren, but left his lights blinking to alert traffic to slow down. He made a quick call to his office and asked his deputy, Stuart, to run a check on the license-plate number. Since the woman wouldn't stop, Wyatt thought the car might be stolen.

He retrieved his ticket book from the glove compartment and climbed out of the patrol car. With quick strides, he approached her, his jaw clenched. He was pissed at her disrespect of the law. He was pissed at her disregard for the safety of others. And he was pissed that his Sunday afternoon had been interrupted.

Wyatt removed his sunglasses and hooked them on his shirt pocket. When he reached her car, he stuck his hand in, turned off the engine and removed the keys, shoving them into the pocket of his khaki slacks. Then he motioned for the driver of the truck to move on.

The driver waved out the window and slowly pulled onto the highway in a gust of diesel fumes. Cars whizzed by, occupants rubbernecking for a better view.

The woman removed an earbud from her ear and pushed her glasses to the top of her head. She glared at him. Her icy-blue eyes were clear, so she wasn't on drugs—he knew the drugged look. They were also red and swollen, as if she'd been crying. That wasn't going to sway him. Speeding wasn't allowed in his county—ever. He had his own personal views about speeders, although he tried not to let them cloud his judgment.

"What the hell do you think you're doing?" she asked with a get-out-of-my-face attitude. "Give me back my keys."

"May I see your license and registration, please?"

"What for?" She flipped back her long, tangled hair.

"You were well over the speed limit, in a business area, too, and you made no effort to stop when you heard the siren."

"Business?" She glanced around at the fields of corn growing on both sides of the highway. "What business?"

He hitched a thumb over his shoulder. "Horseshoe, Texas. You passed the outskirts of town, doing eighty-five, barely missing Mrs. Peabody."

"I didn't see any town or whoever you're talking about."

"Your license and insurance, please." He'd had enough of her attitude.

Jody was waiting.

Tiny lines appeared on her smooth forehead, but she flung a hand to the passenger seat and grabbed a dark tan purse trimmed in red with F's imprinted all over it. Digging through its contents, she found her wallet. It was identical to the purse. Very expensive was his next thought.

Handing it to him, she said, "I'm not taking it out. It was too hard to get into the little slot."

His jaw clenched tighter and he made no move to take the wallet. This lady had a double dose of arrogance. "Remove it, please."

Her eyes narrowed to blue slits as if she was debating the request. Heaving a breath, she struggled with the wallet until the license came out. He noted how careful she was not to break a long, faintly pink fingernail.

He took the license from her, studying the name. Peyton Laine Ross from Austin, Texas. Twenty-eight years old. *Old enough to know better.* "Your insurance, please."

"Officer." She shifted to face him fully, her eyes twinkling with a light he understood well. She was going to try to soften him up by using every feminine wile in her repertoire.

"Sheriff," he corrected her.

"Sheriff" rolled off her tongue like a sweet-cherry lollipop. He could almost taste it, exactly what she'd intended. "I really don't know anything about the car's registration or insurance. My mother takes care of all that. The car is mine and it's insured, if that's what you're worried about." Beneath her lashes, her eyes cast a warm glow that would have weakened most men, but not him.

"Why don't you try the glove compartment?" he suggested, wanting to get this over with so he could be on his way.

"I'm really in a hurry."

"So am I."

She eyed him for a moment and then slid her tongue over her lower lip in a slow, provocative gesture, turning up the glow in her eyes to the sucker level on her male-radar screen.

"I have to get to Dallas as soon as possible." Her gaze moved slowly across his shoulders and chest. "You're a big, strong man and I know you understand."

"Insurance, please," was his response.

The glow dimmed.

Suddenly she flipped back her hair again and looked down at the wallet in her lap. She pulled out a hundred-dollar bill and waved it at him. "Will this make the problem go away? I didn't see your little stop in the road or hear your siren. I was listening to Bon Jovi. You understand, don't you?"

Shock seared whatever patience he had. A frown worked its way across his face. "Are you bribing me?"

She batted her eyes. "Of course not. It's a compromise. You take the money and I'll be on my way. That will make us both happy."

Damn woman! Why did she have to make this so difficult? His Sunday afternoon was now shot to hell. This lady had one heck of a surprise coming her way. He took the money, stuffed it into his shirt pocket and opened her car door. "Get out of the vehicle, please."

"What?" Her voice screeched like a petulant child's. "You took my money."

"For evidence. You're under arrest for speeding and trying to bribe an officer of the law. Now get out of the car."

"You can't do this." She spat the words, her face set. And she didn't budge.

"Get out of the car." His voice matched his mood. Determined. Angry. And slam-damn out of patience.

Her expression locked in petulant mode, she slid out.

She was pretty, very pretty. As his dad would say, she was put together on a Sunday morning when God was in a good mood and the angels were singing in the background. A natural beauty, for sure—one that was enhanced by high maintenance. Big city, class and style flitted across his mind. Her slim, yet curvy body came up to his shoulders. He wasn't sure why he was noticing those things. She was just another woman, and a very arrogant one at that.

Then he became aware of what she was wearing—a silky silver creation that looked like a bridesmaid's dress. Evidently she was headed to a wedding. He purposely avoided looking at the tempting cleavage peeping above the bodice. The hem of the dress fluttered around her ankles. Jody would call it a frou-frou dress.

She stomped her foot. "Do you know who my mother is?"

Her defiant words poked through his thoughts. "No. Can't say that I do."

"She works for the governor of Texas and she'll have your badge for this."

He met her eyes. Five minutes ago, he was inclined to be lenient. Now he didn't want to hear her excuses. "You have the right to remain silent, anything you say can and will he held against you in a court of law. You have the right—"

"You bastard." The heat of her words stained her cheeks and tightened her perfect features.

He spared her a brief glance and continued her Miranda rights. When he finished, he asked, "Do you understand your rights?"

"Do you understand my mother will have your job?" she fired back.

He swallowed a curse word and tucked his ticket book under one arm. With a gentle nudge, he pointed her toward his squad car.

"What are you doing?" She stumbled trying to see his face.

He pulled his hat lower and opened the door to the back seat. "Get in."

"I will not." Her eyes flashed a warning. "Just write me a ticket and I'll be on my way."

The roar of the traffic was deafening, but he heard every word. "I might have been prepared to do that if you hadn't tried to bribe me. That's a serious offense and I don't take it lightly. Now get in the car."

The hot Texas sun caused suffocating waves of heat to roll from the asphalt, yet they stood there eyeing each other like two foes ready to do battle. He'd made up his mind. He wasn't going to relent. This woman needed a dose of reality.

She stuck out her chin. "I have a right to call my mother, you big, overbearing oaf."

"When we get to the jail, you may call whomever you wish, but not out here." Cars continued to whiz by, the exhaust fumes mixed with the heat billowing around them.

"Jail!" The color drained from her face and he saw the first flicker of fear on her face. But it was only fleeting. Anger quickly overshadowed it. "I'm not getting in that car!"

From years of experience, he knew there was only one way to deal with people like Peyton Ross—show her he meant business. He unhooked the handcuffs from his belt.

"You're not…" She took a step backward.

He reached for her hand and snapped a cuff on her delicate wrist. Her skin was soft and satiny. He hadn't touched skin like that in a long time. Quickly he dismissed the sensation. He was an expert at masking his emotions. "Yes. I'm cuffing you."

Before she could react, both wrists were in the cuffs. "As the saying goes, we can do this the easy way or the hard way. Evidently you prefer the hard way." Taking her arm, he angled her toward the open door.

Eyes blazing, she jerked away from him. "Don't touch me, you bastard. You lowlife country bumpkin. You'll pay for this." Even as she blasted him in a voice hot enough to boil water, she lifted her skirt, revealing slim ankles in high heels, and slid into the car.

He slammed the door on her diatribe, threw his book onto his seat and walked back to her vehicle, where he gathered her purse and iPod, as well as a small overnight bag from the floor.

The interior of the car was white leather, and a delicate scent of gardenias reached his nostrils. Gardenias? Not a scent he would associate with the fiery hellcat. Something more exotic came to mind, like Opium or Chanel.

Now why would he think that? He wasn't personally interested in the woman.

He searched the vehicle and didn't find any other valuables, so he headed to his car. He slid into the driver's seat, placing her things on the passenger's side.

"You can't leave my car out here," she told him through the steel-mesh guard that separated the back seat from the front.

"I don't plan to," he replied, picking up his cell and punching out a number. "Bubba, there's a red Lexus coupe on the northeast highway. Please pick it up—we're impounding it."

"Damn, that's an expensive car. Did you catch a drug dealer?" Bubba asked with his usual overactive curiosity.

Wyatt sighed. "Just take care of the car. I'll get with you later."

"Sure thing, Sheriff."

Bubba was one of the Wiznowski family, and he owned a gas station and wrecker service in Horseshoe. Bubba had tried several times to become a deputy, but he never passed the physical because his six-foot-four-inch body weighed more than three hundred pounds. He spent too much time at his grandmother's bakery. But he did help out when Wyatt needed someone to watch the office.

Silence filled the cab, and that was fine with Wyatt. He'd had all of her mouth he wanted. Placing his glasses on the dash, he glanced at his watch. He was late. Jody would be calling. Damn, damn!

Damn Peyton Ross for ruining his Sunday.

Chapter Two

Wyatt's office and the jail were next to the courthouse. A covered walkway connected the two buildings, which had been built in the late 1800s. While there had been updates, basically the two structures stood as they had for years.

He parked the car and got out to open the back door. For a moment he thought Ms. Ross wasn't going to budge. Then without a word, she scooted out and he guided her into his office. The fight seemed to have gone out of her. He hoped that meant she realized the seriousness of her situation.

They went through the room and down the hall to the jail. The tap-tap of her high heels on the concrete floor echoed through the quiet space. After removing the cuffs, he opened the cell door and she walked in, the soft rustle of her gown annoying him for some reason. As the steel bars clanged shut, she jumped, and her eyes brimmed with fire.

"You bastard. My mother will have your hide."

"So you keep telling me."

Her cheeks reddened. "I want my phone."

"Hey, fancy lady," Zeke called from the next cell, his bearded face pressed between the bars to get a closer look. "Ya got a fella?"

"Cool it, Zeke," Wyatt said. "And leave the woman alone. She's not interested in you or marriage."

Zeke was in for "drunk and disorderly". He lived alone in the woods along the Brazos River. Every now and then, he came into town, looking for a wife. Zeke wasn't known for his bathing habits and he probably didn't even own a toothbrush. When women saw him, they ran the other way. Then Zeke would drink and become violent, accosting women, and Wyatt always had to lock him up to give the people of Horseshoe some peace.

The Wilson brothers were in the next cell, and they were a rough lot. The two families with eight kids lived in a three-bedroom trailer deep in the woods. Honest work wasn't for them. They'd run a chop shop until Wyatt closed it down, and now they were into growing and selling marijuana. Wyatt had a feeling the judge was going to throw the book at them this time.

"Wyatt, that's not fair," Leonard complained. "We can't see her."

"Yeah, Sheriff, that's discriminatin' or somethin'." Leroy had to make his views known.

"I'll inform your wives of your complaints when they come to make your bail."

"Ah, c'mon, Sheriff. You know Velma's as mean as a wasp."

"Maybe you should remember that, Leroy, before you go gawking at other women," Wyatt replied. "Now settle down." He walked out before he lost all his patience.

Stuart stared at him, bug-eyed. "Sheriff—" he nodded toward the cell "—that's a woman."

"Notice that, did you?" Wyatt sat at his desk, trying to ignore the astonishment on Stuart's face.

"But we don't have facilities for women."

"We do now." He reached for a pen. "What did you find out about the license number?

"It's on your desk." Stuart pointed to the papers. "I was going to call, but I heard you drive up."

Wyatt scanned the information. The car was registered to Peyton Laine Ross from Austin, Texas. It wasn't stolen and Ms. Ross had no outstanding tickets, warrants or prior convictions. So what had happened today to make Ms. Ross break the law?

Stuart jerked his thumb toward the cell. "Is that Peyton Ross?" His voice was a whisper, as if he didn't want anyone to hear him.

"Yes."

"What did she do?"

As Wyatt filled out the paperwork, he told his deputy what had happened on the highway.

"She tried to bribe you?" Stuart's eyes opened even wider.

"That's about it." Wyatt pulled the hundred-dollar bill from his pocket.

"Gosh darn, that's a lot of money. The last time I saw one of those was when I graduated from high school. My grandpa gave it to me."

As Wyatt fingered the bill, a slight whiff of gardenias lingered. With a frown, he handed the bill to Stu. "Label it for evidence. The judge will be back from his vacation on Wednesday to decide her fate. In the meantime, I'll set her bail."

Since the population of Horseshoe was under two thousand, Wyatt took over setting bail when the judge was out of town.

Stuart slanted his head toward the jail. "But, Sheriff, we have some rough characters back there."

"I know." He studied his pen. He didn't feel right leaving Peyton Ross locked up with Zeke and the Wilson brothers, but what was he to do? She'd broken the law and he couldn't cut her any slack just because she was a woman. But he needed to do something.

"Get some blankets and see if you can hang them from the

bars to give her some privacy. That will keep the guys from gawking at her. But first, please get her case and purse out of my car." Wyatt leaned back and reached into his pocket for his keys, pulling out Ms. Ross's keys, too. He threw the squad car keys to Stuart.

Stuart deftly caught them and glanced over his shoulder. "She sure is a looker, isn't she?" The deputy, like Bubba, had an avid curiosity, and Wyatt wasn't going to stoke it.

He laid Ms. Ross's keys aside and continued to fill out the papers.

There was a slight pause, then Stuart asked, "What's she wearing? It looks like a ball gown or something."

"Get the items out of my car, please," Wyatt repeated without looking up.

Stuart was Horseshoe-born and raised, just like Wyatt. At five foot ten, Stuart was thin and wiry and strong, thanks to his workouts every morning at the school gym. He took his job seriously, but he tended to be a gossip and Wyatt tried to discourage that every way he could. In a small town, it was typical, though. There were very few secrets.

Stuart charged toward the front door and soon returned with Ms. Ross's things. He stood there, fidgeting.

"Blankets, Stu," Wyatt prompted.

"Oh, sure." The deputy hurried to the back room.

Wyatt opened Ms. Ross's case to make sure she didn't have a weapon. Silky, feminine things beckoned. A daring, tantalizing scent filled his nostrils and he wanted to slam the case shut. It reminded him of Lori. Not the scent, but the clothes. Undergarments that he'd enjoyed removing… He closed his eyes tight to block the memory.

It didn't help. Lori's memory was in his heart. And it ached. Ached for her. Ached for them.

Quickly he searched Ms. Ross's bag and wondered why the woman needed so many cosmetics. Finally, satisfied, he picked up her things and walked to her cell. The other prisoners were lying on their cots. Using his key, he opened the steel bars and stepped in.

She sat on the edge of a cot, her face flushed, her eyes mutinous.

He placed her case and purse beside her. "You can use your cell phone to call whomever you wish. Or you can use our phone."

"Am I supposed to say thank you?"

His eyes caught the blue fire of hers. "An 'I'm sorry' would be nice."

"For what?"

"Do you not comprehend what happened this afternoon?"

She folded her arms across her breasts. "I'm sure you're going to enlighten me."

He sucked in a breath. "For the record, you were speeding and almost struck a pedestrian. You did not acknowledge the siren or stop when I motioned you over. And you tried to bribe a sheriff. We may be country bumpkins around here, but most of us know how to obey the law. Most of us respect it, too."

She bent her head and was silent. That shocked him. He expected fireworks. Her demeanor prompted him to ask, "Do you want to tell me why you did those things?"

Her head shot up, her features a mask of seething fury. "Go to hell."

Now he had the fireworks. This lady did not want help. At least he'd tried. "My deputy is going to put up some blankets so you can have some privacy, in case you want to change your clothes. When you need to use the bathroom, a deputy will escort you to the one down the hall. The judge will be here on Wednesday for your hearing. I've set your bail."

"Wednesday!" Alarm bracketed her eyes. Finally he was getting through to her.

Before he realized it, she'd leaped from the cot and grabbed his arm. "Wednesday! You have to be kidding! You can't leave me in this hellhole until then. That's insane. *You're* insane!"

Her fingers pressed into his skin and a forgotten longing shot up his arm and through his system. He had to get away from her.

"You bastard. You country-bumpkin bastard. You'll pay for this. You'll—"

He opened the cell door, stepped out and slammed it shut, the sound resonating in the confines of the concrete walls like a gunshot. He felt a moment of remorse at the terror in her eyes, a terror shrouded in anger and fear. But he'd tried to talk to her and it hadn't worked.

She'd broken the law. Now she had to pay.

PEYTON GRABBED her phone and punched her brother's number. She'd show the high-and-mighty sheriff. He'd regret the day he ever put her in handcuffs.

The weird guy in the cell across the aisle leered at her, his face pressed between the bars. A cold chill scooted across her skin. He reminded her of a bum searching through trash cans on skid road. He licked his lips with a smacking sound. Good grief. She turned away, willing Quinn to pick up.

Pick up, pick up, she silently chanted.

Finally she heard his voice. "Where the hell are you?"

Evidently he'd seen her name on his caller ID. "I need your help."

"You're calling the wrong person, Peyton. Since you skipped out on Mom's wedding, I'm not doing anything for you. Mom was terribly worried and blaming herself for your selfish behavior."

A twinge of hope pierced her chest. "She didn't marry him?"

"Oh, so that's what this little ploy was all about." She could almost see him nodding his head, the way he did in the courtroom. He was a brilliant defense attorney, and if anyone could get her out of this mess, he could. "You thought Mom would be so distraught over your disappearance that she'd cancel the wedding?"

She took a deep breath. "Quinn, I really tried, but I couldn't watch her marry another man."

"Mom has a right to a life. Dad's been dead five years and it's time for us all to move on, especially you."

Peyton bit her lip. Quinn didn't understand. No one did. Her father had been her hero, her best friend, and losing him had shattered everything she'd believed about love and life. She didn't understand how Quinn and her mother could move on so easily.

But she did need to apologize to her mother. "I'd like to talk to Mom."

"No can do."

"Why not?"

"I'm not letting you upset her, Peyton. She's happy and getting ready to go on her honeymoon. I will tell her you're fine, so she won't worry. And do not, I repeat, do not call her on her cell. Let her be happy."

Peyton started to argue like she usually would, but she turned and saw that guy leering at her again. It brought her dire situation to the smack-dab middle of her messed-up life. She had to get out of here.

"Quinn, I need your help."

"You said that before. What's going on?"

"I'm…I'm in jail." Remembering how she'd gotten here warmed her cheeks again. Damn that straitlaced sheriff.

"For what?"

"Speeding."

Her brother sighed. "Peyton, they don't lock people up for speeding."

"Well…" She squeezed her eyes closed, hating to admit the next part and not sure how to explain it to her brother. But Quinn knew her better than anyone.

"You know I've been upset since Mom started dating Garland Wingate six months ago," she said.

"That's no big secret."

"I couldn't believe she was serious." Peyton's voice wavered and she hoped Quinn understood she didn't mean to hurt her mother.

"How many times did I tell you she was?"

"I know. I was in denial. No one can take Dad's place. No one."

"Then, damn it, why did you agree to be a part of the wedding?"

"I didn't want to lose my mother but…but I couldn't go through with it. I sat in my bedroom, decked out in my bridesmaid dress, staring at Dad's picture. In that moment I knew I couldn't be a part of the wedding. It would be a dishonor to him, so I bolted for the garage, fresh air and freedom."

"Very mature, Peyton."

"I had planned to call Mom."

"Why didn't you?"

She winced, knowing what she had to say was going to sound awful. She said it, anyway. "I called Giselle, instead, and she said the sorority sisters were having a big party in Dallas and what I needed was some fun, liquor and sexy guys. It sounded good to me at the time. That way I could forget what Mom was doing."

"Again, a very mature move."

"Stop being so sarcastic." She took a quick breath. "It wasn't easy. As I drove, the tears started and I couldn't seem to stop them. I knew what I was doing was wrong, but I couldn't stop that, either. So I put an earbud in my ear to tune out my conscience."

"I almost feel sorry for you."

"Please, Quinn."

"So what happened?"

She rolled the scene around in her head, searching for the right words. The sheriff of this stop-in-the-road town certainly wasn't in her plans. She honestly hadn't heard the siren and when he'd motioned her over, she thought he was after the truck and wanted her out of the way. She'd never realized she was driving so fast, and then his big bad attitude had rubbed her the wrong way.

"Peyton, are you there?"

"Yes," she mumbled, not believing she'd been so stupid.

"What did you do?"

She dredged up her last morsel of courage. "I tried to give the cop, sheriff or whatever he is, money to let me go."

"You did what?" Astonishment shot through the phone. She could almost hear the reprimand that was about to erupt.

"Why the hell would you do that?"

"Giselle told me she never gets tickets because she flirts with the cop and shows some cleavage. If that failed, then money always did the trick. Cops barely make minimum wage and need extra cash."

Oh, why had she even thought of Giselle's ploys? The sheriff hadn't even noticed her cleavage. And the sheriff of Nowhere, Texas, turned out to be *honest*.

"And you listened to that airhead? She's always getting you in trouble."

"Stop being so judgmental and get me out of here."

"Where are you?"

"I don't know, somewhere between Austin and Dallas." What had that snotty sheriff called it?

"I need a name, Peyton." His astonishment turned to irritation. "Weren't you paying attention? Or do you even care? You just expect me to drop everything and figure out where you are and solve your little problem. Typical Peyton."

He made her sound selfish and spoiled. Someday soon she might have to admit the truth of that, but not now. "Horse something. Yes, that's it."

There was a long pause on the line. "You know what, Peyton, why don't you get comfy? After what you did to Mom, I'm not running to your rescue. It's time for you to grow up and start thinking about someone besides yourself for a change. Give me a call when that happens. And you might check out the name of the town in the process."

"You wouldn't dare—"

The sudden dead silence on the line told her he would. She had the urge to throw the phone. With restraint, she sank onto the lumpy cot and slowly started to count.

One. Quinn would come.

Two. Quinn wouldn't leave her in this backwater town, whatever it was called.

Three. She slammed the phone onto the cot.

Pride wouldn't let her ask the sheriff the name of the town. From her position, she had a very narrow view of the sparse office, but she could see him sitting at his desk writing something. He'd removed his Stetson hat. A wayward lock of dark hair had fallen across his forehead. His khaki shirt stretched across broad shoulders. The sun coming through a window caught his badge and it winked at her like a caution light.

She noticed all that a little too late. He was a no-nonsense, straightforward lawman, a mix between Clint Eastwood and Jimmy Stewart. Some women might find that attractive, but she found him a bore and a bully.

As she scooted back to sit on the bottom of the bunk beds,

she wondered if the sheet was clean. The steel bed had a lumpy mattress, pillow and a dirty brown blanket. A roach skittered across the grimy concrete floor. She jerked up her legs, shuddering. She had to get out of here. Fast.

She'd show that cocky sheriff.

He wasn't keeping her a prisoner.

Quinn would come. He always did.

Chapter Three

Wyatt wasn't sure what to do with Ms. Ross. She'd made her phone call, so why wasn't someone calling to arrange her bail? His plans were to release her if she promised to return on Wednesday for the hearing. But so far he'd heard nothing from her family.

And it was getting late. He had to call Jody.

Before he could punch out the number, his daughter bounded in with Dolittle, her yellow Lab, trotting behind her. She was dressed in her customary jeans, sneakers and a T-shirt, her short blond hair clinging to her head like a frilly cap. She looked so much like Lori that it squeezed another drop of sadness from his heart. Her eyes were like his, though, dark brown with flecks of green.

"Hey, Daddy, what's taking so long?" She rested her elbows on his desk and cupped her face, those big eyes sparkling like the rarest of gems. He'd never thought it possible to love someone so much, so deeply, but he did—the same way he had loved her mother. There was nothing on this earth he wouldn't do for his daughter. He'd give his life for her in a heartbeat. She was everything to him and would be until the day he died.

He swallowed the lump in his throat. "I have a situation here at the jail." Glancing outside, he saw her bicycle. "Does Grandma know where you are?" Usually his mother called when Jody was on her way to his office.

Jody shrugged. "Grandma doesn't know where I'm at half the time."

"Really?" He leaned back in his chair.

"Shoot." Jody snapped her fingers. "Ramrod says I'm the sharpest knife in the drawer and sometimes I cut my own self."

Everyone in town knew Jody and she wasn't in any danger. But it was against the rules for Jody to leave the house without permission. His daughter spent too much time at the local barbershop owned by Virgil and Ramrod Crebbs. They were old cowboys who had grown tired of the long hours in the saddle and had moved to town. They opened the one and only barbershop. Jody loved to hear their tales and she'd picked up their lingo.

Disciplining his daughter was hard. She had him wrapped so tight around her little finger that he let her get away with just about everything. He had to be stronger where Jody was concerned.

How many times had he told himself that? Just last week he had been called to the school because Jody had punched a boy in her class. The boy had told her she was a pretty girl. Apparently, those were fighting words. Jody was a tomboy and refused to admit she was a girl. Although the two of them has talked about this often Jody stuck to her stance that she was just Jody, not a girl.

He sucked in the fatherhood department.

Jody was a loner and that bothered him. She didn't have friends her own age—all her friends werc adults. He had to address that problem soon, too.

Dolittle came around the desk and nuzzled Wyatt's leg.

Wyatt scratched the dog's head. "So you left the house without telling Grandma?"

"Well, Daddy, it was like this." Her brown eyes grew serious and he just wanted to kiss her sweet, pixie face. "Grandma was having her Sunday poker game and she was telling Gladys that she needed to get her cataracts removed because she couldn't see squat. You know how Gladys hates it when Grandma tells her what to do. They were having a loud argument about mind-your-own business types of things when I shouted that I was going to see what was keeping you so long."

"I see." Wyatt realized he had no control over any of the women in his life. His mother played the organ in church on Sunday mornings and then played poker with her friends in the afternoon.

Gambling was illegal in Texas, so he'd told them they couldn't play for money. But the winner bowled free on Tuesdays and also got a free lunch; the others paid, at least that was what his mother told him. Half the time he didn't know what the ladies were up to, and most of the time he'd rather not know. He'd prefer not to have to lock up his own mother.

Trying to look as stern as possible, he pointed a finger at Jody. "Next time, make sure Grandma hears you."

At the firmness of Wyatt's voice, Dolittle became rigid, on guard. They'd had him since he was a pup, and they realized early that the dog was lazy and did very little, hence the name. But he was protective of Jody and he'd fight a lion for her.

Wyatt rubbed the dog's head, letting him know that no one was hurting Jody.

"Sure. No problem," Jody replied. "Are you ready to go now? Virgil says the catfish are biting today. He says he caught one this big." She stretched out her arms as far as she could.

"Virgil tells a lot of fish stories."

"Uh-uh, Daddy." Jody shook her head vigorously. "Virgil doesn't lie."

Stuart came out of the back room with an armload of blankets. Jody ran to him. "Whatcha doing, Stuart? It's too hot for blankets."

Stuart leaned down and whispered, "We have a female prisoner and I'm fixing her some privacy."

"Oh." Before Wyatt could stop her, Jody darted down the hall to the jail. He was instantly on his feet. But Dolittle was in the way and he almost tripped over him.

Jody stared though the bars at Ms. Ross. "Why are you dressed like that?"

"Stop gawking, little girl," the woman said. "This isn't a sideshow."

Jody's face puckered into a frown. "I'm not a girl. I'm Jody."

"You look like a girl to me."

"*You're* a girl," Jody said.

"Well, Jody-with-a-gender-issue, go away and leave me the hell alone."

Jody put a hand over her mouth. "Oh, you said a bad word."

"Like I care. Go away, brat."

Jody placed her hands on her hips. "You're not nice and I hope my daddy lets you rot in here."

"Do you not understand the meaning of 'go away'?"

Jody stuck out her tongue. Wyatt pulled her away and led her back into the office. "You know you're not supposed to speak to the prisoners."

"What did she do, Daddy?" Jody pulled free of his hold and looked up into his face.

Wyatt didn't plan on answering that question. Jody didn't need to know. He glanced at the clock. Almost four. Time to get in a little fishing.

"Stuart, my daughter and I are going fishing."

"Yay!" Jody jumped up and down.

"If anyone calls about Ms. Ross, call me on my cell and I'll come back and sort it out."

"You gonna leave me here with her?" Stuart's left eye twitched, which always happened when he was nervous.

Wyatt reached for his hat. "Is that a problem?"

"No…well…" Stuart held his hand over his mouth so Jody couldn't hear. "What if she attacks me when I hang the blankets? I don't want to hit a woman."

Wyatt glanced at his watch. "Lamar's shift starts at five so wait until then. Surely the two of you can handle one woman."

Stuart nodded his head. "Yes, sir."

Wyatt pointed to the bail book. "Leroy's and Leonard's wives are coming in with bail money, so let them go then."

"Sure thing, Sheriff." Stuart winked at Jody. "Catch a big one, little bit." Everyone in town called Jody that.

Wyatt shook his head as he walked out the door. One feisty blonde had his office turned upside down.

Hopefully her powerful mother would show up soon with a lawyer and Ms. Ross would be out of his hair.

For good.

FOR THE FIRST TIME in years, Wyatt wasn't enjoying the fishing. He kept wondering what was going on at the office. And he wondered about Peyton Ross. Why was she so defiant and angry? She seemed to have class and beauty, but on the inside she was like rebellious teenager determined to prove something. He wondered what.

At dusk he drove Jody home and went to check on things at the jail. Jody wanted to go with him, but he wouldn't let her. She spent too much time there, too. Soon he'd have to set rules for his child—and enforce them—or she was going to be the wildest kid in Horseshoe.

Lamar was at the desk when he went in. He immediately jumped to his feet. In his early twenties, Lamar was somewhat overeager. He always tried to please and at times it could be a little tiring. But Lamar was dedicated to his job, and Wyatt trusted him completely.

"How's it going?" Wyatt asked, sinking into his chair.

"Okay, I guess. Leroy and Leonard are gone. Zeke is a pain as usual, demanding to be released."

"And Ms. Ross?"

Lamar scratched his head. "She refused supper. Said she doesn't eat garbage. She had a few choice words to say about you, too. That woman has a bad attitude, but she's real easy on the eyes."

Wyatt ignored that. "Has anyone called about her?"

"Not a soul."

Damn. Where was this powerful mother? He got up and made his way to her cell. Blankets were hung haphazardly from the bars, but none over the door. He could see inside. She sat on the bottom bunk in pink capris, a sparkly tank top and sandals. She'd changed her clothes, but the expression on her face was the same—rebellious.

"Would you like to try your mother again? We haven't heard from anyone." He was as cordial as he knew how to be, just as his parents had taught him.

"Don't worry, you will," she replied with a lift of a finely arched brow. "And you can kiss that shiny badge on your chest goodbye. My mother will have you for breakfast."

He rubbed his jaw, feeling a five-o'clock shadow. Again he wondered what had happened to make her so bitter. "Have you ever heard that you can catch more flies with honey than with vinegar?"

"Sorry, I'm not up on your little country sayings, but you might try catching some of these roaches in here. I'm sure locking me up in such a dump is breaking several laws, not to mention some health violations."

His cordial attitude went south. Wyatt tipped his hat. "Good night, Ms. Ross."

"Go to hell," she shot back.

THE NIGHT WORE ON and Peyton kept glancing at her watch. *Quinn will come. Quinn will come.* By ten o'clock she knew he wasn't coming. A tear rolled down her cheek and she quickly slapped it away. She wouldn't cry. That Mayberry sheriff would *not* make her cry.

The tiny lightbulb cast depressing shadows in the cell. This couldn't be happening to her. She'd planned to drink and party with her sorority sisters until she could no longer see her beautiful mother with that man. Oh, how could she marry Garland Wingate!

He was so different from her scholarly, gentle father. Garland owned an oil company and wore cowboy boots. So uncouth. Much like the sheriff of this one-horse town.

What was she going to do? Quinn would probably let her stew overnight and be here in the morning. But what if he didn't? He was angry with her and had a right to be. She needed to talk to her mother and apologize. Then this terrible nightmare would end.

She still had her phone. The sheriff had forgotten to retrieve it. Ignoring her brother's warning, she punched in her mother's number. It rang once and went to voice mail. Of course. Her mother was on her honeymoon.

Anger flashed through Peyton and she fought it. There was nothing she could do now. Her mother had married Garland. She started to leave a message, but what would she say? How could she excuse her behavior? She couldn't even explain it to herself.

Good manners. Good behavior. She'd left those behind the moment she'd decided to run.

Slowly she placed the phone on the cot and glanced around at her dismal surroundings. *Ohmygod!* She was in jail—locked up. It suddenly hit her like a slap in the face and it stung. She had to find a way out of here. She wasn't a criminal.

"Hey, fancy lady, ya sleep?" the man named Zeke called.

"Leave me alone," she said.

"Ya got a fella?"

Could she be in any more of a backwater? "Shut up."

"I got a place on the river, even got runnin' water."

Was this idiot for real?

"I wanna marry up and I'd be good to ya, might even put in a bathroom for ya. Whaddaya say, fancy lady?"

"The only thing I want is to get out of this jail."

"I git ya outta here."

That caught her attention. "How?" She immediately wanted to snatch the word back. Had she completely lost her mind?

"I got ways."

"Just leave me alone, okay?" The last thing she wanted was to get involved with this crazy person. She felt something touch her ankle and she jumped, tucking her feet beneath her on the cot. It was probably a roach. Her skin crawled with revulsion. How was she going to survive this night?

"Hey, Lamar," Zeke shouted. "I feel sick."

"Go to sleep, Zeke," The deputy shouted back.

"I'm gonna throw up. The food must a been bad."

"You're trying my patience tonight."

Loud thuds echoed on the concrete. The deputy was coming to the cell.

She got to her feet and peered out to see what was going on. She had a feeling the man wasn't sick. What was he up to?

"I got a fever, too. Feel me."

The deputy stuck in his hand to touch Zeke's forehead. As he did, Zeke's thick arm snapped out and grabbed the deputy around the neck, yanking him up against the bars. The deputy jerked, coughed, sputtered and slid to the floor in a crumpled heap.

Ohmigod! What did the man do? Peyton wondered if Lamar was alive. He was so still. She swallowed back a scream.

Zeke crouched down and through the bars reached for the keys on the deputy's belt. A sly smile crossed his bearded face as he withdrew them. Then he reached for the gun and stuffed it into the waistband of his worn, dirty jeans. Quickly he inserted the key into the lock and opened the door.

He stepped over the deputy's body and, to her horror, unlocked her door. *No! No!* She took a couple of steps backward and looked for something to use as a weapon. There was nothing but her high heels. As he advanced on her, a glint in his bloodshot eyes, she bent down to pick one up.

Before she could reach it, he grabbed her around the neck and jerked her up against his body. "I told ya, fancy lady, I git ya outta here."

Her scream wedged in her throat and she couldn't breathe. The man had a foul body odor and he smacked his lips in glee. His shaggy, grayish beard brushed against her cheek like a Brillo pad, and chills skipped across her skin.

He dragged her toward the door and she realized he was taking her with him. She kicked back with her feet and connected with his shins, but it didn't even faze him.

"Let me go, you beast!"

"Ya want outta here, so I'm taking ya to my place. Ya belong to me now."

"What?" Her body grew weak with fright. She wanted out of here, but not like this.

"The sheriff won't find us, might not even look. He'll be glad to see the back of ya, fancy lady."

Her breath came in shallow gasps as he lugged her struggling body to a back door.

Where's the sheriff? went repeatedly through her mind like a prayer before a disaster. He was her only hope. Just moments ago she never wanted to set eyes on the man again, but now he was the only person she wanted to see.

And she didn't even know his name.

The door came open easily and Zeke hauled her outside into the sultry summer night. The scent of crepe myrtles wafted on the soft breeze, the delicate fragrance pleasant and embracing, a sharp contrast to the terror that gripped her. She blinked at the bright floodlight that illuminated a parking area. To the left, her car and a rusty old truck were enclosed inside an eight-foot-high chain-link fence.

Zeke dragged her toward the double gates. She tried everything she could to slow him down. She dug in her heels and then bit his arm, but to no avail. His heavy arm around her neck was strong and suffocating.

When they reached the gates, he yanked out the gun and fired at the chain. Her pounding heart jammed against her ribs at the sound and her ears rang. She held on to her composure, though. Barely. Hysterical screams were right there at the edge of her throat. Someone would hear the shot and come, right?

She held on to that thought.

Zeke kicked open the gate and jogged toward the truck, still tugging her along. She realized this was her last chance and she gave full rein to the screams.

He clamped a filthy hand over her mouth while opening a door and lifted her onto the seat as if she weighed no more than a rag doll.

"Let me go, you maniac!"

"Stop it." He pointed the gun at her. "Or I'll shoot ya."

Her throat closed up.

"Git over," he growled.

In a moment of clarity she realized this really was her last chance. She quickly scooted over torn upholstery to the passenger's side, intending to open the door and run like hell. The truck was strewn with trash and stank of rotted food and urine. Paper cups, newspapers, dirty clothes littered the floor and the seat.

She held her breath against the stench as she searched for the door handle. There wasn't one—just a hole where one used to be. *No! No!* Frantic, she ran her hand over the inside of the door one more time. Nothing.

"Gimme yer hands."

She twisted around and saw he was in the truck and the door was closed. In his big hands was a small rope. She froze.

"Gimme yer hands," he said again.

"No." She backed against the door.

Before she could do anything else, he grabbed her hands and whipped the rope around them with lightning speed. With one movement he jerked the rope so tight it cut into her skin. She had to force herself to take deep breaths.

Fear held her paralyzed as Zeke fiddled with some wires beneath the dash. After a second the truck sputtered to life.

Zeke let out a chilling victory laugh and slammed the stick shift into gear. The truck was backed into a parking spot, so when he hit the gas pedal, they shot through the gate and out into the night.

Panic rose in her anew. She had no idea where he planned to take her. The sheriff would come, she kept telling herself.

She'd told herself that earlier, she realized with annoying insight. She'd thought Quinn would come. And he hadn't.

All her life her father had made sure she never wanted for anything. All she had to do was be his little princess, the light of his life. He took care of all her problems, all her worries. She was loved, pampered, safe and secure.

But now…

For once in her life she was on her own.

WYATT COULDN'T sleep. He didn't feel right leaving Ms. Ross in the jail. Zeke was as obnoxious as a man could get and he'd likely taunt Ms. Ross all night long. Where was Ms. Ross's important mother?

He always trusted his gut instincts and something told him he was needed at the jail. Maybe it was his conscience. He slipped into jeans, boots and grabbed a short-sleeve shirt. Checking the jail one more time would give him some peace of mind and then maybe he could sleep.

His mother, Maezel, known to everyone as Mae, was in the living room, watching an old Elvis movie. She was a fanatic about the man—there was Elvis memorabilia all over the house. Wyatt complained about it so much that she now kept most of it in her room. His mother was eccentric, to say the least. His childhood had been colorful and he knew every song Elvis had ever sung. Wyatt refused to talk about his middle name.

"Mom, what are you doing still up?"

She rose to a sitting position. At sixty-eight, his mother was still in good health, though prone to bouts of depression, when she went silent. Those silent spells got him, so he'd turn up the Elvis music and soon she was back to her old self.

Pushing permed, short gray curls from her forehead, she replied, "I could ask you the same thing."

"I have to go back to the jail."

With her eyes on the TV, she said, "Jody says you have an uppity city lady locked up."

"Yeah. I have to check on her."

"Go. Go." She waved him away. "I don't want to miss this scene with Ann-Margret."

She'd seen the movie a hundred times at least, but that was his mother—living in Elvis Presley's time zone.

"If Jody wakes up, tell her I'll be back as soon as I can."

"She never wakes up," Mae said, her eyes glued to the screen. *"Viva Las Vegas."*

He placed his hat on his head with a wry grin and headed for the back door.

His father, John Wyatt Carson, had died ten years ago of lung cancer; he'd smoked two packs a day until a month before his passing. He was set in his ways, but he'd been a loving, caring father—although sometimes, especially when Wyatt was a teenager, a little stricter than Wyatt would have liked,

His father had been a highway patrolman and believed in rules and discipline, as Wyatt did now. But somehow Wyatt wasn't very good at disciplining his own child.

His mother was very little help in that area. Mae Carson was an easygoing person who lived in the moment. Discipline wasn't high on her list of priorities.

She'd lost a son to meningitis when the boy was just five years old. That was before Wyatt had been born and his father had told him that his mother had never been the same afterward.

For a solid year she'd grieved and no one could reach her, his dad had said, and then one day she started singing "Kentucky Rain" and "Are You Lonesome Tonight?" She'd listened to Elvis's records over and over, and Wyatt's father had let her be. She'd found her solace.

Over the years his mother's eccentricity increased. But these days she was content, and Wyatt was grateful to have her in his life to lean on when things got rough. She looked at the world a little differently, but who was to say what was right and what was wrong?

She was probably the main reason he'd moved back into his childhood home. He needed a little of her kind of insanity in his life, Elvis songs and all. He slid into his car and headed for the jail.

There'd been too much dying in the Carson family. Maybe that was why he was so lenient with Jody. He wanted their days to be happy because life could be snatched away without a moment's notice. And he wanted every memory to be treasured.

When he walked into his office, he heard a faint moan. A flicker of apprehension shot through him. He ran into the jail and saw Lamar lying on the floor. Zeke was gone and so was Ms. Ross. Damn it all to hell!

Kneeling, he felt for a pulse. When he found it, a sigh of relief escaped him. Lamar moaned again and Wyatt helped him sit up.

"Are you okay?"

Lamar rubbed his throat. "That bastard choked me."

"Zeke?"

"Yeah."

With Wyatt's help, Lamar staggered to his feet. They walked into the office and Lamar flopped into a chair.

"What happened?" Wyatt asked.

"Zeke said he was sick and had a fever. I…I fell for it. He had me around the neck before I knew it. I'm…I'm sorry, Wyatt."

"Did he take Ms. Ross?"

Lamar went still. "Is she gone?"

"Yes."

"I heard them talking." Lamar rubbed his throat.

"About what?"

"I… Oh, Sheriff…" Lamar was shaking and his skin was a grayish color.

"Take a deep breath," Wyatt coaxed while reaching for his cell to call Judy Deaver, the nurse. Since Horseshoe didn't have a clinic, they depended on the nurse for minor emergencies.

"Judy, this is Wyatt. I need you at the jail immediately."

"Be right there."

"Keep taking deep breaths," he told Lamar.

Next he called Stuart and didn't waste words. "Get to the jail now." He had a feeling time was of the essence.

Lamar was about to slide out of the chair, so Wyatt urged him to stand, wrapped an arm around his waist and guided him to a cot in the back room.

"Relax and try to breathe normally."

"My throat hurts and…and I can barely breathe."

Judy came through the door with her bag.

"Back here," Wyatt called.

"What happened?" she asked, taking Lamar's pulse.

"Zeke near choked the life out of him."

She spared Wyatt a glance. "When are you going to do something about that man?"

"Tonight," he replied. He'd let Zeke Boggs get away with too much because of his diminished mental capacity, but kidnapping a prisoner was way over the line. Or at least he assumed she'd been kidnapped. Ms. Ross might have talked Zeke into letting her go. Then he'd have two prisoners on the lam. Either way, it wasn't good for his department.

Stuart charged through the door, still stuffing his shirt into his pants. "What's happening?"

Wyatt reached for his rifle in the gun cabinet. "Zeke assaulted Lamar and escaped. Ms. Ross is gone, too. I don't know if they're together or not, but I will find out."

"Holy crap! We've never had a jailbreak."

That didn't sit well with Wyatt, either. "Call Bubba and get him to watch the office. Use your truck with the four-wheel drive and head to Earl Boggs's place and let him know you're going through his property to get to Zeke's place. Tell him I'm going through the back way on horseback. It should be faster. I'll meet you at Zeke's."

"Okay."

Wyatt handed him a rifle. "Be careful and watch your back."

The only way to get to Zeke's quickly was through the Daniels property, which bordered Boggs's land. As Wyatt spun away from the office, he reached for his cell and poked out Tripp Daniels's number.

Tripp answered on the second ring.

"This is Wyatt. I hate to bother you at this time of night, but I need a fast horse."

He and Tripp were friends. They went to school together for a time when the Carsons had moved to nearby Bramble to take care of his mother's mother. Tripp was a rodeo rider, but he'd retired and settled down with a wife and a family.

"You got it."

Wyatt liked that about Tripp. No questions. He knew Wyatt wouldn't ask unless it was important. "See you in about ten minutes."

Wyatt swerved onto the dirt road that led to the Lady Luck Ranch, hoping his instincts were right and Zeke had hightailed it to his shack and moonshine still on the river. He also hoped he hadn't taken Peyton Ross with him. That would mean, though, that Ms. Ross had persuaded Zeke to unlock her cell and let her go. She would be an escaped prisoner. A huge knot formed in his gut. And it had a name. Peyton Ross.

He had a feeling he was going to rue the day he'd ever set eyes on the woman.

Chapter Four

Wyatt drove past the large, two-story colonial house to the barn and corrals. A light was on in the barn, so he knew Tripp was there. He grabbed his rifle from the back seat and climbed out.

As he did, Tripp emerged from the barn, leading a brown mare with a blaze of white down her face and one white-stockinged foot. Tightening the saddle cinch, Tripp said, "That didn't take you long. What's the rush?"

"I had a jailbreak tonight."

Tripp lowered a stirrup and turned to face Wyatt. "Damn. So who are you after?"

"Zeke Boggs."

Tripp stepped away from the horse with a frown. "He was in Bramble a couple of weeks ago scaring all the women to death. Horace locked him up and then escorted him out of town."

Wyatt shoved his rifle into the scabbard on the saddle. "We've all been lenient with Zeke, but this time he's crossed a line. He helped a female prisoner escape and I have to find him fast."

"What!"

Wyatt put his left foot in the stirrup and swung into the saddle. "Do you mind if I go through your land to get to his shack?"

"Of course not. Do you need any help?"

"No. I can handle Zeke. Thanks for the use of the horse. I appreciate it."

"Her name is Blaze—she's a workhorse. She won't let you down and she'll carry you right through those brushy areas."

"I owe you."

"You sure do," Tripp said. "I had my arms wrapped around the most gorgeous woman in the county."

"Give Camila my best." Blaze was prancing, ready to run. Wyatt held her back, glancing at Tripp's leather house shoes. "Those are really bad for your cowboy image." With that, he shot out of the yard, but not before he saw Tripp's wide grin.

PEYTON WASN'T SURE how long they had been driving, but it seemed like hours. She kept pushing on the door with her body in hopes it would come open. Tumbling out onto the road seemed a good alternative to her current situation. It was probably rusted shut, though. The rope cut into her skin and it burned and hurt like hell.

They were now on nothing more than a dirt track, bumpy and narrow. Her insides were being jostled like something in a blender and she felt nauseous. The truck's one headlight picked out a heavy thicket. Where were they?

In her mind the answer came a little too quickly— *somewhere where no one will find you.*

She swallowed hard to block her thoughts. *The sheriff will come.* Although he annoyed her, he appeared competent.

The stench in the truck was getting to her. Could one expire from odors? She'd never thought much about death before her father had become ill. She didn't like the idea of it then and she certainly didn't like it now. How could she get away from this horrible man?

Suddenly the beam of the headlight exposed a clearing with a small dilapidated shack and an attached lean-to. A creek or river flowed nearby. Two rusty trucks were parked to the side and weeds flourished around them. Junk and clutter filled the yard, from an old washing machine to a pile of cans and bottles.

Definitely a place where a body could be buried without anyone ever finding it. A nervous hiccup slid down her throat.

Zeke stopped the truck and reached under the dash to disconnect the wires. The engine sputtered away. And then there was silence.

"This is it," he said proudly. "My home. I need a woman to take care of it."

A bulldozer would take care of it. The words died in her throat. To get away from him, she was going to have to use some of the tactics Giselle had talked about. They hadn't worked on the sheriff, but Zeke was a simpleton and she had a feeling she could work that to her advantage.

She shifted to look at him. "Please let me go. I don't know anything about your ways or how to live in the wild. I'm a city girl." She dropped her voice to a soft pleading. "Please, just let me go."

And if you don't, I'll start screaming and lose what composure I'm managing to maintain.

"No," he replied stubbornly. "You're mine now."

She bit her lip to keep the screams inside her. But she wasn't giving up. She just had to bide her time.

Zeke opened the door and got out, looking back at her. "Git out," he ordered.

She scrambled out, eager for fresh air. The rope cut deeper with each movement, but she was able to stand on her feet, her lungs soaking up the night air untainted by filth.

She held out her hands. "Would you please undo these? The rope hurts."

He shook his head. "No. You'll run away."

"Where would I go?" She glanced around at the thick woods.

He didn't respond, but turned and grabbed her arm, leading her toward the shack. No way was she going inside. Once she did, she knew there would be no escape.

She staggered on purpose. "I feel faint," she murmured, and sank to the ground.

"What's wrong with ya?" He squatted beside her, peering into her face. She forced herself not to recoil from his closeness.

"I don't know. I just need to rest."

And to think.

He waited.

Peyton took a long breath, grateful for this reprieve. Any other time the moonlight would have been breathtaking as it bathed the forest in an effervescent glow. The water rippled pleasantly, crickets serenaded and the place was eerie and peaceful at the same time. But there was nothing peaceful about her situation. How would she get away from him?

"This is all mine," he said again in that proud tone." My brother's wife and her family live farther west, but this land is mine and they can't take it. If you marry up with me, it'll be yours, too."

Responding would be like talking to the trees, so she didn't waste her energy.

"I make a lot of money selling my moonshine. I got the best still in the county, all copper. You can have the money, too."

The man was off his rocker. Suddenly an idea came to her. She moaned and held her tied hands to her face. "I feel like I have to throw up. Please undo the rope." She had seen him use this little trick and she hoped it worked.

Without a word, he removed the rope and she had to restrain herself from cringing as his thick fingers touched her wrists. She flexed her fingers. "Thank you." The sheriff had said something about using honey instead of vinegar. Well, she was going to honey ol' Zeke to death.

"Are ya better?"

"I could use some water, please."

He pointed to something that looked like a well pump. "There's plenty."

Was he serious? Without a doubt he was. "Would you get some for me, please? I'm so weak."

He grabbed her arm in a viselike grip and hauled her to the well. "Don't try anything. Remember I still got the gun."

Oh, God! *Stay calm.*

When they reached it, she knelt and her capris soaked up the mud around the well. Zeke pumped the handle and water spurted out. She cupped her hands and pretended to drink, but let the flowing water run through her fingers and onto her clothes.

"See I told ya I got water. Now let's go inside. Ya can cook us up somethin' to eat."

Like hell. She stood and linked her fingers together, making a two-handed fist. It was now or never.

"Let's go," he said as he stepped closer.

With every ounce of strength she had, she swung her clenched hands at Zeke's face. There was a loud pop, skin connecting with skin, and to her surprise Zeke went down. She took off at a run for the woods, not looking back.

THE THICK WOODS and brushy undergrowth impeded Wyatt's progress. But Blaze was everything Tripp had said—a real workhorse. She picked her way through the thicket easily, never faltering. Luckily there was a full moon to light the way.

The heat was oppressive in the deep woods and every breath of air was a godsend. The mosquitoes were thick and he wished he'd taken the time to put on a long-sleeve shirt. But his only goal now was to reach Zeke's. He feared for Ms. Ross's safety.

He finally reached the Brazos and he urged Blaze faster as they followed the riverbank toward Zeke's property. Reaching the clearing, he dismounted and looped the reins around a drooping tree branch. He pulled the rifle from the scabbard and moved toward the shack.

As he drew closer, he saw Zeke's truck and stopped. Zeke was here. Was Ms. Ross? An owl hooted, breaking the unending silence. Something rustled in the bushes and Wyatt scanned the perimeter of Zeke's cluttered yard. Where was he?

He heard a moan. It sounded like a wounded animal. As Wyatt watched, a form rose in the moonlight. Zeke. He rushed forward and pushed Zeke to the ground, holding the rifle on him.

"Sheriff," Zeke blubbered in surprise, holding a hand to his head.

With a foot on Zeke's chest, Wyatt asked, "Where's Ms. Ross?"

"Who's that?"

"The woman you took from the jail," Wyatt replied.

"The fancy lady?"

"Yes. Where is she?"

Zeke rubbed his head. "She hit me."

Wyatt removed his foot, not in the least surprised.

"Where is she now?"

"Don't know. Don't want a woman who hits."

"Why did you take her in the first place?"

"She wanted out of jail and I git her out."

"Why didn't you let her go?"

Zeke frowned. "'Cause she's mine."

Wyatt exhaled deeply. "Zeke…" Just then, headlights darted though the woods. A door slammed and Stuart charged into the clearing with his gun drawn.

"Over here!" Wyatt called, and pulled Zeke to his feet. "Cuff him," he said to Stuart.

As Stuart snapped handcuffs onto Zeke's wrists, Wyatt asked again, "Where did the woman go?"

"Don't know. Don't care," Zeke muttered. "She hit me."

Stuart looked at Wyatt. "What do you think?"

Wyatt glanced toward the woods. "I think she's out there somewhere."

"What do you want me to do?"

"Take Zeke and lock him up, then get together a posse. We have to find her."

"Are you staying here?"

"Yes. I'll start searching."

Stuart grabbed Zeke's arm. "What were you thinking? You can't just take a woman. That's kidnapping. Now she's lost out here."

"Don't care."

On the way to the truck Stuart continued to reprimand Zeke, but Zeke stuck to his "don't care" reply. Ms. Ross had shattered his illusion of what a woman should be. Wyatt thought Ms. Ross was good at shattering illusions.

Wyatt removed his hat and wiped his forehead with his arm. Hot sweat trickled down his back. Why did Ms. Ross have to speed through his town?

Where was she? The woods were big and she could be anywhere. He settled his hat on his head, swatted a mosquito and cupped his hands around his mouth.

"Ms. Ross, can you hear me?" he called. "Zeke is gone. You're safe. Ms. Ross!"

Zip. Nada. Nothing.

Heaving a deep sigh, he walked toward his horse. He had to find her. Ms. Ross was going to be the death of him.

PEYTON RAN and kept running. She had to get as far away as possible. Brush and branches scratched her arms, legs and face, but she didn't stop. The madman was behind her—with a gun. Her breathing became labored and sweat coated her body. She still refused to stop.

Her foot caught on a tree root and she fell headlong to the ground. She spit out a leaf and dirt. Unable to stop herself, she began to cry—tears rolled from her eyes and sobs racked her body. She curled into a fetal position and gave into them.

For about five minutes.

Then she sat up and wiped at her face with her dirty hands. The darkness surrounded her like walls. Something stung her arm and she scratched it. Another sting. Mosquitoes. Damn it! Just what she needed.

Through the weblike branches of the trees she could see the moon, but the trees kept the light from finding her. She was truly alone. Quinn had let her down. The sheriff had, too.

A rustling sound trapped her attention. What was out there? she wondered, shivering in the stifling heat. Her new companion, fear, was right there in her chest. She knew nothing about survival. She'd been pampered and sheltered. Nightmares like this happened to other people.

How had this happened to her?

She had caused it.

The truth of that hit her in the chest. She was her own worst enemy. At twenty-eight she had thrown a hissy fit because her mother was remarrying. Quinn and her mother had told her to grow up.

Growing up like this was hell.

She slapped another mosquito and stood, resolute now. She had to prove that she wasn't a cream puff and that she could take care of herself without Quinn's or her mother's help. She would survive this. All she had to do was keep eluding Zeke. By morning the sheriff would discover she was missing and start a search for her. He had to, she reasoned. He was the sheriff.

Dusting off her clothes, she listened closely in case Zeke was lumbering through the woods after her. A thud-thud sound was unfamiliar. It could be Zeke. She had to keep moving. She turned and froze.

A hog, the size of a walrus, grunted a few feet away. It had to be a wild boar because he sure looked different from the pigs she'd seen on TV and in movies. His skin wasn't slick and smooth, but dark and straggly with longish hair. Its snout was longer, too. It emanated a sharp sound that wasn't friendly.

In a blink of holy hell the hog lowered his head and charged her. She screamed and dove for a tree, grabbed a limb and climbed faster than she ever could have imagined. Her foot slipped and she gripped another branch. She heard and felt a snap. The limb gave way and before she knew it she was falling.

No! No!

She hit the ground as a gunshot rang out, echoing chillingly through the trees. Scrambling to her feet, she was off again even though every muscle in her body protested. Zeke would not catch her.

"Ms. Ross!"

She knew that voice. She swung around and glimpsed the sheriff astride a horse. Moonlight glistened off the rifle he held in his hand, and even though shadows lurked around him, the sight was comforting. He dismounted. "Ms. Ross," he called again. "It's the sheriff. You're safe."

Chapter Five

Wyatt was taken aback, but he held and comforted her as if she were Jody, even with the rifle in his hand. But she wasn't Jody. Ms. Ross's body was soft and curving into his in a familiar way. Her trembling only made his reaction to her more powerful. He didn't understand—he had no interest in Ms. Ross, other than as a prisoner.

"You're safe," he told her, stroking her matted hair.

"Is…is…the hog dead?"

"Yes."

She rubbed her face against his shoulder. "Where…where's…?"

"Zeke?"

She nodded her head.

"My deputy is taking him back to jail. Are you okay?"

She pushed away from him in one angry movement. "Do I look okay? I'm filthy from head to toe. Mosquitoes the size of 747s have attacked my body. My arms and face are scratched and my wrists have rope burns. That…that man…"

Ms. Attitude was back with a vengeance. Still, he had to sympathize with what she'd been through.

"Maybe the size of a small Cessna."

"What?" She blinked.

"The mosquitoes are not quite as big as a 747."

She slapped one on her arm. "I beg to differ." She scrubbed at her arms. "I can still feel that…that man's horrible touch. And I prefer the mosquitoes."

"Did he hurt you?" Wyatt asked, feeling a moment of inadequacy. He hadn't been able to protect someone under his care.

"Of course he hurt me. He dragged me from my cell and wouldn't let me go. He tied my hands and threatened to shoot me. He's crazy. I'm going to sue you and this inept town for everything it's worth."

That hit Wyatt on the right side of wrong. His department had failed her, but she was at fault, too. She wasn't the innocent victim she thought she was.

"You encouraged him."

"What?"

"You told him you wanted out of jail. Zeke is not too bright, as you may have noticed. He thought if he made your wish come true, you'd be grateful."

"I didn't ask him to break me out of jail!" she yelled. Her irate voice echoed though the trees.

"What did you ask him?"

She shoved back her hair, which was tangled around her face. "I'm not saying one more word to you. You can speak to me through my attorney."

"Fine," he retorted. "I've been waiting for over twelve hours for someone to speak to about your bail, but no one has shown. Why is that?"

He couldn't see her eyes clearly, but he knew they were shooting sparks at him. He jammed the rifle into the scabbard. Placing his boot in the stirrup, he swung into the saddle.

"I'm going back to Horseshoe. Are you coming?"

"Like I have a choice."

Removing his boot from the stirrup, he held out his hand. After a second, she took it and he hauled her ornery ass up behind him.

At that moment she saw the dead boar and the dark blood oozing from its neck. "Oh, gross." She turned her head in the other direction.

He kneed the horse and they were off.

Wyatt followed the river and then veered west toward the Daniels property. Nothing was said. Her arms clasped him around his waist a little tighter than he would have liked, but he didn't say anything. No conversation suited him fine where Ms. Ross was concerned.

Her head bobbed against his back. "Don't go to sleep," he warned. "You might fall off."

"I'm just so tired," she replied without her usual bite.

"So you're talking to me now?"

"Yes. But I'm still suing you."

"Go ahead. I don't have a lot and Horseshoe is a very poor town. You wouldn't get much."

"I'd get revenge."

"Would that make you happy?"

"Damn right. It's been a nightmare ever since you arrested me."

"Somehow it's my fault you were speeding, breaking the law and endangering lives."

"You didn't have to lock me up."

"You tried to bribe me."

He waited, but there was no comeback.

"When are you going to take responsibility for your actions and stop blaming other people?" he asked.

The question caused a twinge within Peyton more powerful than the siting of one of those 747 mosquitos. The correct answer was, "Right here, right now," but she wasn't going to give the sheriff the satisfaction. She didn't understand, though, why it was so hard for her to admit she'd been wrong.

Maybe because she never had to before.

And she didn't have to now. Quinn would get her out of this mess and she would never have to set eyes on the sheriff again. That had been her modus operandi in the past…but this time her conscience was kicking in. She didn't understand that, either.

The moonlight and easy rhythm of the horse was hypnotic. She was so tired and she wanted so badly to go home. But home was different now. *He* would be there—her mother's new husband.

As exhausted as Peyton was, she was aware of the strong muscles of the sheriff's back. His stomach was the same—abs of steel. The man must work out. In his profession, she supposed it was required. Her nose was an inch from his neck, and a manly scent mixed with leather and sweat tickled her nose—not a laughing kind of tickle, but a evocative, sensual one that stirred the senses.

But not *her* senses. He wasn't her type and she wasn't attracted to him in any way. She didn't go for he-men. Still, she had to acknowledge that he was a very virile, attractive man. In bowling terms he'd be a ten pin, definitely a strike.

A moment of nostalgia hit her. Her father had been an avid bowler, the only physical thing she'd ever remembered him doing. When she'd started dating, he'd ask, "Is this gentleman a seven or eight pin?" She'd make a face and reply, "A three or four." She vowed that the day she found a ten, she'd marry him.

She'd never rated a man that high. Until today. She wondered if she had injured her head when she'd fallen out of the tree.

They rode right into a barn. A light was on and she blinked against the brightness. As her eyes adjusted she saw a dirt floor, stalls for horses, bales of hay, a hayloft and a wall where bridles and ropes hung. Saddles and blankets were draped over wooden horses. The smells of hay and leather filled her nostrils.

"You can get off," the sheriff said, and she realized she still didn't know his name.

She swung her leg over the backside of the horse and slid to the ground. She staggered for a moment, but quickly regained her balance.

With one easy movement the sheriff dismounted and she became aware of his height and the breadth of his shoulders. He was slim and muscled in all the right places. He wore jeans and a shirt with a gun belt strapped around his hips. Clint Eastwood popped into her mind again. She felt dizzy.

"What's your name?" she found herself asking.

He glanced over his shoulder as he removed a rifle from the saddle and placed it against a large round post holding up the loft. "Why?"

"So I'll know who I'm suing."

He quickly undid the straps on the saddle. As if the saddle was a toy, he slung it over a wooden horse and then looked at her. "Wyatt Carson."

She lifted an eyebrow. "You mean, like Wyatt Earp?"

"Yes." His lips tightened for a second and then he shrugged. "What can I say? My dad was an Old West enthusiast." He grabbed a brush and walked to the horse and began to brush her coat. "You did good, girl, real good," he said to the horse.

"You're talking to the horse?"

"Yep. Blaze did a stellar job getting me to Zeke's fast and safely." He began to lead the horse out of the barn to a corral.

"Oh, no."

He swung back to her. "What?"

She held up her dirty hands. "I broke four nails and I just had them done."

"Now that should be a crime," he replied dryly continuing out of the barn with the horse.

She didn't consider that funny. Filth coated her skin and clothes. She shook dirt and leaves out of her hair. Her Prada sandals were caked with mud. Damn! She needed a bath. And her freedom.

From Wyatt Carson and this insane town.

He strolled back in, picked up the rifle and headed for the big doors. "Let's go."

She followed, and when he stopped unexpectedly, she ran into his rock-hard back. As he flipped off the light, he said, "Watch where you're going."

Darkness shrouded them now, and unable to stop herself, she stuck out her tongue at his retreating back. Was the man always this serious? And so aggravating? She hurried to keep up with his long strides.

His car was waiting outside. He placed the rifle on the back seat and slid into the driver's side. She opened the door on the passenger side and hopped in. She smelled coffee and spied a half-empty cup of it in the console, along with a small bag of M&Ms. Her stomach grumbled and she realized she was hungry—very hungry. She could ask for the candy, but pride wouldn't let her.

The sheriff poked out a number on his cell phone. "Stu, I found her. We're coming in." After he clicked off, he started the car and drove toward a dirt road.

"Where are we?"

"Lady Luck Ranch."

"Where are we going?"

"Jail."

Fear trumped her hunger pangs. She couldn't go back to that place. She licked suddenly dry lips. "Will Zeke be there?"

"Yes."

She'd tried every trick she knew on the sheriff and none had worked, so she decided to use a little honesty. Maybe he'd appreciate that. "Please don't make me go back there. Zeke scares me."

He stopped at a cattle guard, the headlights showing a paved road ahead. "Ms. Ross, where is your mother?"

She squirmed. "Does that matter?"

"Yes." He shot her a glance. "If she will pay your bail, you can go home tonight, or I should say this morning." He paused for a second as if to let that sink into her head. "Where is this mother you've been throwing in my face?"

"I still—"

"Where is your mother?"

She jumped at the sharpness of his voice and knew she was going to have to tell him. She clenched her hands into fists. "She's on her honeymoon."

"Excuse me?" He turned slightly in his seat to face her. "So you were headed to the wedding? Is that why you were in such a hurry?"

She started to fib, which she never had a problem doing before, but something about this lawman made her think twice. "Not really, but it doesn't matter. I called my brother, who's a lawyer, and I'm sure he'll be here in the morning."

"Why isn't he here now?"

Why couldn't he stop asking questions? She resisted the urge to squirm again. It felt as if he had a built-in lie detector. Only the truth would suffice.

"He's upset with me because I skipped out on my mom's wedding. He's trying to teach me a lesson, but he'll come. He always does."

"So he gets you out of a lot of trouble?"

"Not serious stuff. Sometimes my sorority sisters and I party too heartily. Things like trashed hotel rooms, noise complaints and one time in Bloomingdale's my friend mentioned that a clerk had a big ass and then the woman wouldn't wait on us, so we just walked out with the merchandise."

"And the lawyer brother gets everything swept under the rug."

She was immediately on the defensive. "Is that relevant to my situation now?"

"Yeah. You're of the opinion that you can get away with anything. Someday you'll have to take responsibility for your actions, without big brother," he replied, swerving left on the blacktop road.

Peyton had nothing to say. The sheriff had effectively burst her bubble of bravado. For the first time shame edged its way into her conscience.

Wyatt knew he had a problem. He couldn't take her back to the jail with Zeke in the next cell. What was he supposed to do with her?

"Please don't take me to jail."

That soft, pleading voice hit him square in the chest. From the short time he'd known the woman, he knew she didn't beg. She was scared. And no wonder after the ordeal she'd been through. His department was at fault, so he had to make it right. There was only one place he could take her—his home.

Everything in him shouted no.

"Are you sure your brother will be here in the morning?" As he asked the question, he realized again that it was already morning. He could put up with her for a few hours and then she'd be out of his hair and out of Horseshoe.

Until the hearing.

But that was out of his hands. Her family would pay a big fine and Peyton Ross would be just a bad memory.

Chapter Six

Wyatt took the cutoff for Horseshoe. Nothing else was said and he knew he didn't have any other options. His mother wouldn't care. She welcomed everyone into her home. For years he'd been thinking he needed to buy a house for him and Jody, but like so many things he'd kept putting it off.

When he'd first returned to Horseshoe after Lori died, he'd updated his mom's house by installing central air and heat and completely repainting the whole place. Every now and then he thought he should do something "girly" for Jody's room. But she always put the kibosh on that idea faster than he could get the words out of his mouth.

He glanced at his watch—5:30 a.m. His mother usually got up around five. It depended on how late she was up watching a movie. He turned left on Mulberry Street and whipped into the backyard where he always parked his patrol car.

"Where are we?"

"My mother's house."

"Oh. You're going to let me stay with your mother?"

"I live here, too."

"Oh." This time there wasn't as much enthusiasm in the word. Her face worked into a frown. "You live with your mother?"

"Yes. My daughter and I do."

"You have a kid?"

"It doesn't matter!" he snapped. "This is the only solution I have. For the next few hours you'll be on the honor system. You do know what that is, don't you?"

"Well—" she tucked tangled hair behind her ear "—I do, but you better give me your version. I have a feeling it's different from mine."

He bet it was. "I trust you to do as you're told and be cordial to my mother and my daughter. I trust you not to try to escape or encourage anyone else to help you. If you do, I'll just issue a warrant for your arrest. Are we clear?"

"Yes."

He unbuckled his gun belt and wrapped the belt around the holster.

"Do you always wear a gun?" she asked.

"When I have escaped prisoners." He opened the glove compartment and placed the gun inside and locked it. He was a breath away from her, and as grubby as she was, she still managed to project femininity. He found he was eager to pull away; she was too close for comfort. "Now, let's go inside and see how my mom feels about having you here."

As they reached the back steps, the kitchen light came on. He opened the door and allowed Ms. Ross to enter the house before him.

His mom, in a flowered robe, her gray hair mussed, turned from the coffeepot on the counter. "Oh, you're… Oh, we have company," she said.

"Mom, this is Peyton Ross. Do you mind if she stays here a few hours?"

Mae took in Peyton's appearance. "What happened to you, hon?"

"Zeke broke out of jail and took Ms. Ross with him," Wyatt answered for her. "Her brother is coming this morning to pay her bail and I can't have her at the jail with Zeke."

"'That's All Right, Mama'." His mother waved a hand and then looked at Ms. Ross. "Do you like Elvis?"

Oh, God, couldn't his mother give Elvis a rest for one day? She was in the habit of answering with a title of one of Elvis's songs. Sometimes it could get confusing.

As it was for Ms. Ross now.

Wyatt leaned over and whispered. "Just say yes."

"Yes," she said.

"Good. I'm making coffee and it'll be ready faster than Elvis can gyrate his hips." The woman winked. "Maybe not that fast and certainly not that enjoyable."

"Okay." Ms. Ross glanced warily from his mother to him. "I'd really like a bath."

"Wyatt, show her where the bathroom is," his mother replied before he could.

"Mom, could you do that, please? I need to check in with Stuart and pick up Ms. Ross's things."

"Come this way," Mae said. "You can use anything. Just don't touch my Elvis soaps."

"Okay," she replied, still sounding puzzled.

"Ms. Ross," he said, and she turned, her eyes huge.

"Remember our discussion."

She nodded and he saw how exhausted she was. Her hair was matted with dirt and her skin was caked with it. Red blotches from mosquito bites dotted her face and arms. Guilt scraped his conscience at his inability to protect her. There was nothing he could do about that now except ensure her safe return to her family.

IN A GLANCE, Peyton took in the bathroom. It was small and clean with the basics, but the tub had an Elvis Presley shower curtain, and Elvis soaps filled a decorative Elvis dish on the vanity. Evidently Wyatt's mother was an Elvis Presley fan. Could the people in this town get any weirder?

She didn't care. She'd be gone in a few hours. Opening a cabinet, she pulled out a blue, fluffy towel. She was glad it wasn't an Elvis towel. While the tub filled, she stripped off her dirty clothes and soon lowered her weary body into the warm water. Heaven.

There was shampoo in a caddy hanging from the shower-head. Not her usual brand, but it would do. She scrubbed her hair and her body, trying to erase the remnants of this awful night. Then she lay in the tub, just enjoying the luxury. The dirt under her nails seemed permanent, much like the gardener's who tended their lawn in Austin. She gave up trying to remove it. A manicure was at the top of her list when she returned to the comfort of her own home.

When the sheriff brought her things, she'd call Quinn to make sure he was on his way. Then she'd phone her mother and apologize. But she still didn't know how she was going to accept her mother's new husband. That might take a while. The first step would be to get her own place. The move was way overdue. She'd been in the process of looking for a condo when her father had become ill. Afterward she couldn't leave. He'd needed her.

Her eyelids drooped and she realized how tired she was. She sat straighter. It wouldn't do to fall asleep in the tub. Grabbing the towel, she climbed out and rubbed her body dry. She had mosquito bites and scratches all over her, and they all itched and burned. The sheriff would pay for this.

A bubble of laughter rippled from her throat. She was sure he was quaking in his cowboy boots. How many threats could she hurl at him in one day? She was sure his broad shoulders could take anything she dished out. Opening the medicine cabinet above the sink, she searched for something to apply to the bites. Benadryl cream—just what she needed.

She sat on the white and blue linoleum squares and rubbed cream on each bite. The stinging stopped almost immediately. She continued with the scratches and rope burns.

Thoughts of the handsome sheriff filled her mind and she couldn't seem to stop them. He was like a mosquito bite she couldn't stop scratching. She guessed his age was around thirty-five. Why was a man that age living with his mother? He had a kid, so was there a wife? He hadn't mentioned one.

Leaning her head against the wall, she remembered him saying he didn't have a lot. What exactly did that mean? Did he have financial problems? And why did she care? In a few hours, she'd leave this town and file the memory under "lessons learned."

When are you going to take responsibility for your actions?

Peyton heaved a sigh. Her brother would be here today. Quinn would set the sheriff straight, and she looked forward to that.

Quinn was like a pit bull in a courtroom, fighting for his client's innocence. He'd fight even harder for her. Wyatt was in for a big surprise.

But somewhere in the region of her functioning brain she knew the sheriff could stand toe to toe with anyone, including her brother.

WHEN WYATT RETURNED, his mother was sitting at the kitchen table, drinking coffee. He'd brought Judy with him, wanting Ms. Ross to have medical attention.

"Hi, Judy," his mom said. "How about a cup of coffee?"

"Thanks, Mae. I'd love one."

"Where is she?" he asked, feeling a bit of trepidation at the quiet.

His mom jerked a thumb toward the bathroom. "She's still in there."

"What? What the hell can she be doing this long?"

Mae shrugged. "Bathing, I suppose."

Wyatt headed for the bathroom, wondering if she'd managed to slip out the front door. He was pretty sure she wouldn't try anything, but he could be wrong.

He knocked lightly on the door so as not to wake Jody. "Ms. Ross, I have your things."

There was silence for a moment and then he heard movement. Relief surged through him and that surprised him. But he was glad she'd kept her word.

The door opened a crack and she stood there in nothing but a blue towel that made her eyes appear even bluer. Her hair was wet and hung in strands around her face. Silky-looking skin dotted with cream peeped above the towel. Sleepy blue eyes gazed back at him. Raw, primitive and all-male emotions roused his lower abdomen and below. Even the bites on her face and neck didn't diminish her appeal.

Or his reaction to her.

Peyton Ross was like the pinups he used to hang in his locker in high school—pinups that Lori had taken down. At the thought of his wife, all those raw emotions eased into exactly what they were—an appreciation of the female form.

He handed her the case. "Here're your things. Your wallet is in the safe at the office—just thought I'd remove temptation."

Frowning, she held the towel with one hand while taking the case with the other. Her fingers brushed across his and he felt as if he'd been baptized by fire. Baptized like a teenager who'd been touched by an attractive, sexy woman for the first time.

He stepped away and headed for the kitchen and a cup of coffee. Something stronger might be better, though. He was just sleep-deprived, that was all, he kept repeating to himself.

And he missed Lori.

When they'd first married, she'd worn nothing but a towel after her bath and he'd chase her to remove it. Laughing, they'd tumble into bed. Those were wonderful, beautiful memories forever etched into his mind.

And his heart.

PEYTON DUG in her purse for her phone, called Quinn—it went straight to voice mail. *No! No!* She left a terse message and carefully laid the phone in her bag. Don't panic. Quinn just wasn't up yet. She'd try again later.

She noticed her bridesmaid dress stuffed in the bag. Not much use to her now. A moment of after-the-fact, bad-daughter guilt hit her. She ignored it and quickly dressed in white capris and a green-and-white tank top. White lace edged the scooped neck of the top, barely covering her breasts. Was it too revealing?

She held a hand over her mouth to keep from laughing. Before today, she could honestly say that thought had never crossed her mind. But here in Hicksville, U.S.A, she was sure it would be frowned upon. Like she cared. If the sheriff didn't approve of her attire, he could just blow it out his ears. It was all she had, for her other clothes were ruined.

After towel-drying her hair, she picked up her case, tidied the bathroom and returned to the kitchen. Wyatt sat there with his mother and another woman, drinking coffee. Her stomach rumbled, reminding her of her hunger.

"Hon, would you like some coffee?" Mae asked.

"Yes, please." She slipped into a chair and placed her case on the floor.

"Ms. Ross," the sheriff said, "this is Judy Deaver, the town nurse. I'd like for her to take a look at you to make sure you're okay."

"Like hell. No one in this insane town is touching me."

Judy's honey-colored eyes filled with alarm and she got to her feet. "I know you're upset—"

"Upset! I've been kidnapped, brutalized, attacked by mosquitoes and I fell out of a tree."

Judy glanced at the sheriff. "Maybe a trip to the E.R. in Temple would be a good idea."

"Listen, lady, I'm not going anywhere but home to Austin. I'll see my own doctor there." The sooner the better. She just wanted to go home and get away from these weird people.

"Are you refusing medical treatment?" Wyatt asked.

"You got it. I guess you're not such a dimwit."

His body stiffened and fired a full round of angry testosterone her way.

Judy shrugged. "You're on your own with this one, Wyatt. See you later, Mae."

As the door closed before her, Peyton asked, "Was that supposed to mean something?"

"It means... Never mind." He took a gulp of coffee.

"I really don't care." She motioned toward the bathroom. "I left my dirty clothes in there. I wasn't sure where the trash was."

Mae turned from pouring a cup of coffee. "Trash? Hon, haven't you ever heard of a washing machine?"

"I'm sure the clothes are ruined." She wasn't going to admit that she'd never used a washing machine.

"Whatever." Mae placed a white cup trimmed with blue flowers in front of her.

"Thank you." She wanted to ask for a tall vanilla latte with a shot of caramel, but figured that was out of the question. She wondered if milk was out of the question, too. She hate drinking it black, but she was so hungry it might not matter.

She could feel the sheriff's eyes on her. She'd noticed that he'd removed his hat and a lock of dark hair had fallen across his forehead.

"Did you reach your brother?" he asked.

She gripped the warm cup. "He didn't answer. I'm sure he's still asleep. I left a message, though."

"What time does he get up?"

Before Peyton could reply, a little girl followed by a massive yellow dog burst into the room. "Daddy, Daddy!" she cried, wrapping her arms around Wyatt's neck. "Why didn't you wake me? You always wake me."

"Morning, sunshine." He kissed her cheek and all the anger on his face disappeared. "I've been out on a case all night, so I'm running late."

The girl had blond hair, so she must favor her mother, wherever she was. Clearly Wyatt loved his daughter. She could tell by his voice and the way his big hands held her—the same way her father had held her.

"I'm hungry and—" The girl stopped abruptly when she saw Peyton. "What's she doing here? I don't like her."

"This is Peyton Ross," Wyatt told her. "And she's our guest."

"I don't care. I don't want her in our house!"

Wyatt stood with the child in his arms and carried her from the room. Peyton recognized the girl from the jail and she guessed the child had reason to dislike her. But it was a first for Peyton. She was a likable person. At least she had been before her arrest. Now she was bitchy, angry and plain out of patience. And she had to admit she'd been in that bitchy mood when she'd met Jody. A mood brought on by the sheriff, her father.

"Would you like something to eat, hon?" Mae asked as if nothing had happened.

Her hunger overtook everything else. *Oh, yes, mercy me, yes. Food and lots of it.* Meekly, she replied, "Yes, please."

Mae opened a cabinet door. "We have Fruit Loops, Raisin Bran, Cheerios, Grape-Nuts, Honey Bunches of Oats…"

Cereal! She was offering her cereal. Didn't women who lived in the country cook hearty meals? Peyton had been thinking more along the lines of French toast dripping with maple syrup or waffles or pancakes with bacon and sausage. But *cereal!*

"I'll take the honey-and-oats thing," she said before the offer was rescinded.

"The cereal is here, bowls are there." Mae pointed to another cabinet. "Silverware is in that drawer and milk's in the refrigerator. Help yourself. I'm going to get dressed." Then she sashayed out of the room as best as her floppy slippers would allow.

Peyton jumped up and grabbed the cereal and a bowl. It didn't take her long to find a spoon and milk. She paused for a minute at the refrigerator as she spied cheese and luncheon meats. But she would eat only what she was offered. She was going to make Quinn buy her the biggest lunch ever. Maybe steak. Maybe Chinese. Or Italian. She'd never been so hungry.

She had the cereal ready in a moment and took her seat to enjoy it. The dog sat on his haunches, watching her. She ignored him and took a bite.

She was starving, so the cereal tasted like a double-fudge sundae with nuts and a cherry on top. She gobbled it up.

The dog whined. She didn't know anything about dogs. Her father had allergies, so she'd never owned one. Was the animal hungry? Did he want her cereal? Could dogs eat cereal? She didn't have a clue, but he'd have to fight her for it.

She made another bowl and doctored her coffee with milk and sugar. The dog whined again.

Go away.

Instead, the dog moved closer and nuzzled her calf with his nose. She froze. Was he going to bite her? *Go away! Go away!*

But he persisted and looked up at her with expectant eyes. Without a second thought, she reached out and patted his head. That seemed to do the trick. Satisfied, he lay down at her feet.

She stared at her hand and wondered if she should wash it. Hunger blocked out her reasoning. She wiped it on her pants and kept eating.

Voices could be heard in another part of the house. Clearly the sheriff was having a talk with his daughter. The kid didn't have to worry. This houseguest couldn't wait to leave, and she would as soon as possible.

Chapter Seven

"That was very rude, Jody, and I'm not happy with you." Wyatt sat with his daughter on his lap as she burrowed further into his chest.

"Why does she have to be here?" Jody wailed. "She called me a girl and a brat."

"You *are* a girl."

"I'm Jody," she insisted stubbornly.

Someday soon he was going to have to tackle this problem. But right now he had another problem to address. Taking a long breath, he pushed aside his frustration with his fathering inabilities. He reached a forefinger to her chin and turned her face so he could look into her eyes. "Ms. Ross is my prisoner and my responsibility. Zeke escaped from jail last night and took Ms. Ross with him. She's been through a terrifying experience and needs a place to rest until her brother arrives."

"Oh." Jody's eyes opened wide.

"So can I count on you to help me ensure Ms. Ross's safety?"

She nodded, her blond bangs bouncing on her forehead. "Okay, Daddy. I'll help you."

"You have to be polite and courteous, the way we treat everyone who comes into our home."

"She just better not call me a girl or a brat."

"Jody." His voice was sharp, as he'd intended.

"Okay." She lowered her head.

"I mean it, Jody."

She looked up, her eyes sparkling. "I'll be very, very nice. You'll hardly recognize me."

He squeezed her tight to keep from laughing. "I knew I could count on you, sunshine. I love you."

"Love you, too, Daddy."

He stood and set her on her feet. "Let's go see how Ms. Ross is doing."

As they entered the kitchen, they saw Ms. Ross eating cereal. Wyatt cringed inwardly. It was Jody's favorite cereal.

Jody glared at Peyton. "You're eating my cereal." She shook the box. "And now it's all gone."

"Oh. I didn't know. I—"

"It's okay," Jody said, to Wyatt's surprise. "I'll eat Fruit Loops, but first I have to feed Dolittle." The dog and Jody bounded out the door to the long porch across the back of the house.

Wyatt pulled out a chair and faced Ms. Ross. "May I have your brother's number, please?"

She rattled it off and he reached for the pen and notepad in his shirt pocket. "Does he have an office number?" She gave him that, too, with the brother's name and firm. "Hopefully we can finalize things this morning."

"He's not going to let you or this town off easily."

"Yeah." He stuffed the pad into his pocket. "Another thing you keep reminding me."

She licked the spoon and he watched the action for a fascinated second. "It's true."

He rose to his feet, needing to put distance between himself and Ms. Ross. "Bribery is bribery, Ms. Ross, any way you look at it."

She slowly licked the spoon again and he clenched his jaw. She was an expert at provocative gestures.

"So is kidnapping and brutalizing a prisoner."

"The judge will sort it out." He grabbed his hat from the table. "I have to go back to the jail. You're still on the honor system." Walking out, he released a taut breath. Her brother couldn't come soon enough.

As SOON AS the sheriff left, Peyton reached for her phone and called Quinn again. It went to voice mail—again! Where was he? This wasn't like him. He was always connected in case a client needed him. She called his office and his secretary said he was out for the rest of the week.

Why? she kept asking herself. He hadn't told her he was going anywhere. Of course, she hadn't listened that closely. She'd been too absorbed in her own misery. He, on the other hand, had been involved in the wedding plans. Maybe he was taking care of after-wedding details like the wedding gifts and rental table and chairs. But, no—someone had been hired to do those things.

Where in the hell was he?

Mae came back into the kitchen, wearing tan slacks and a pin-striped blouse. Without a word to Peyton, she opened the back door and shouted, "Jody, stop rolling on the grass with Dolittle. Get in here and change your clothes."

"Coming, Grandma."

Mae then looked at Peyton. "Well, hon, I guess you're stuck here for the morning."

"It appears that way."

"After you do the dishes, you can watch TV or whatever. Just don't mess with my Elvis stuff."

Dishes? Was she kidding? She didn't *do* dishes.

The kid came running in, out of breath, the dog at her heels.

"Did you have breakfast?" Mae asked.

"Nope."

Mae opened the cabinet. "What kind of cereal do you want?"

"Fruit Loops."

Mae handed her the box and went to the refrigerator for the milk. The girl sat at the table and ate her breakfast. The pair tended to ignore Peyton and for some reason Peyton felt slighted. But it was for the best. She had no desire to talk to them, either. What she wanted was sleep and a double cheeseburger.

"Do you mind if I take a nap?"

"You can use the sofa in the living room." Mae gestured at the doorway. "But the dishes have to be done first."

Okay. She could put a few dishes in a dishwasher. With her bowl in hand, she headed for the sink and looked for the dishwasher. She didn't see one.

"Where's the dishwasher?" she asked.

Mae lifted an eyebrow. "At the end of your arms."

Peyton bristled. "You expect me to wash dishes?"

"Yes. You have something against getting your hands wet?"

"I resent being treated like a maid." Peyton placed her bowl in the sink with the other dishes and headed for the living room. The room had hardwood floors partially covered with a braided area rug. A piano occupied a spot by the front door. The mantel over a stone fireplace was littered with family photos and Elvis memorabilia.

One of the sheriff with a pretty blonde caught her eye. Obviously his wife, and Peyton wondered where she was. Telling herself it was none of her business, she curled up on the sofa and closed her eyes. Cool air wafted from a vent above her head. The house actually had central air and heat. Now, that was a surprise.

As sleep avoided her, her conscience tuned in, the volume high. The sheriff had said to be cordial and she had blown that, big-time. It wouldn't kill her to wash dishes. She'd eaten their food—if you can call cereal food—so requesting compensation for that was not out of line. She'd been out of line, though. Once again. Still, she couldn't believe they didn't have a dishwasher.

How poor were they?

EVERY EFFORT Wyatt made to contact Quinn Ross met with no results. The woman at his office said he wasn't expected in all week. Ms. Ross's family seemed to be suspiciously unavailable, so he did some checking.

Maureen Ross did work for the governor as one of his assistants. And she did get married on Sunday afternoon in her Austin home surrounded by friends and family. She and her new husband were now on an Alaskan cruise. Quinn Ross was a lawyer—a defense attorney, the worse kind in Wyatt's opinion. He'd seen too many clever ones get hardened criminals off or procure light sentences.

Ms. Ross hadn't lied about any of that. He wondered, though, why her family had deserted her. What had she done?

Stuart walked through from the jail.

"Has Zeke settled down?" Wyatt asked.

"He's still mumbling about being hit."

Wyatt leaned back. "Maybe Ms. Ross has cured him of looking for a woman."

"Yeah. A woman should've hit him sooner and then we wouldn't have a passel of problems this morning." Stu grimaced. "What are we going to do with the guy?"

"I spoke with Thelma Boggs this morning and she'll be here Wednesday for the hearing. I also spoke to the district attorney.

We don't have much recourse this time. Zeke is probably going to be admitted to a mental institution. Mrs. Boggs agrees."

"We let him get away with a lot." Stuart sat in the chair across from Wyatt and yawned. "We should have done something years ago."

"We thought he was harmless."

Stuart yawned again.

"Go home and get some sleep. I can handle the office, and I'll call Bubba if I have to leave."

"Nah. I'm fine. Have you heard from Lamar?"

"He's at Scott & White in Temple, undergoing tests. He might be back by the end of the week. Until then it's you and me. And as I said, Bubba's always willing to help."

Stuart folded his hands behind his head. "What are you going to do about Peyton Ross?"

"Pray her brother shows up, but I'm beginning to have my doubts."

Stuart yawned so wide Wyatt could almost see his tonsils.

"Go take a nap on the cot. I'll wake you when I have to go home."

Without another word of protest, Stuart ambled to the back room. In a few minutes Wyatt heard snoring. He quietly closed the door and stretched.

Damn! He was dog-tired.

And his day had just begun.

PEYTON AWOKE with a start. The sheriff's kid was kneeling on the floor in jeans and a T-shirt, staring at her.

"You snore."

"I do not." Peyton rose to a sitting position. No one had ever told her that before. She was sure it wasn't true.

"You make noises like Doolittle makes. I call it snoring."

"Go away, kid."

"Nope. You're a guest and I have to be nice to you."

"By telling me I snore."

"Your hair's a mess, too."

Peyton frowned. "Are you trying to make me angry?" On reflex, her hand went to her hair. Strands were still damp and tangled. A mess, just like the kid said.

"Nope. I'm being nice."

"Yeah, right." Peyton picked up her phone and checked to see if Quinn had called. He hadn't. Desperation clutched her heart. What was she going to do? She couldn't stay here one more minute.

"Grandma's waiting for you to do the dishes."

Grandma could take a freakin' leap.

She looked at the child with the enormous, mischievous brown eyes. Her hair was cut short and clung to her head in a pixie look. She didn't favor her father, except for the eyes and maybe that stubbornness. Having never been around children, Peyton found them a little unnerving. She never knew what to say to them, so she usually avoided the little critters. But this one was in her face.

How hard could it be to deal with a child? Quinn had told her repeatedly that she was still one, so this should be like stuffing her face with ice cream.

"What's your name?" Peyton had heard it at the jail, but had forgotten.

"Jody. And don't call me a girl or a brat."

The kid had said something like that yesterday. What was her problem? Peyton thought it best not to press the issue. She had enough troubles of her own.

She got up and went into the kitchen for her case. Another gray-haired woman sat at the table with Mae.

"Is that her?" the woman asked.

"Yes, Gladys, that's our houseguest."

Gladys squinted through her thick-rimmed glasses. "Too good to do dishes, huh?"

Peyton picked up her case and went back to the living room and Jody. Unzipping her bag, she searched for her hairbrush, found it and then attacked the tangles.

"Why do you put that on your toes?" Jody asked, staring at Peyton's French pedicure.

Her hand stopped in midair. "It's nail polish. I like it."

"Why?"

Peyton thought for a minute. "It makes me feel pretty, like a woman."

"Yuck!"

"I enjoy feeling like a woman."

"Why?"

"Because—"

The slamming of a door interrupted them. "Daddy's back." Jody jumped up and ran for the kitchen.

Peyton sat completely still, going over her options. She had other relatives she could call, but the humiliation would be unbearable. Explaining her actions to people who would judge her just wasn't on her to-do list.

She could call some lawyer friends of her brother's. They dealt with criminal's every day and knew the drill. But that, too, would entail more embarrassment than she was willing to endure.

No. She'd gotten herself into this mess and she could get herself out—some how. At the moment she didn't have a clue. She'd have to take her chances in this weird town.

She looked up and the sheriff stood there, his dark gaze somber.

Chapter Eight

Wyatt eased into the recliner across from her. "We have a problem, Ms. Ross."

She scrunched up her nose. "Could you please call me Peyton? Ms. Ross sounds like my mother."

He gritted his teeth. "As long as you're in my custody, you're Ms. Ross."

"Do you ever relax?"

"Ms. Ross, you're brother is unreachable for a *week*. Do you have anyone else you can contact?"

She pulled up her knees and wrapped her arms around them. "Yes, but I'd rather not."

"Why?"

"I'm not in a mood for a lecture."

"Maybe you need one."

"And maybe you need better security at your jail."

He gritted his teeth again. By the time Ms. Ross left his jurisdiction, his teeth would be nubs. "The hearing is on Wednesday morning at ten. This is Monday. I have no place to hold you for the next two nights."

"I'm fine right here."

"That's my point. You've worn out your welcome. My mom

is not pleased with your attitude. I thought we discussed the cordial part—did I not make myself clear?"

"She expects me to wash dishes."

"And somehow that is out of your realm of capabilities?"

She made a face. "There's no dishwasher."

He scooted to the edge of his chair and the edge of his patience. The last place he wanted Ms. Ross was in his home, but again he was out of options. "Here's the deal. You apologize to my mother and wash whatever she asks you to wash. You keep your mouth buttoned and be grateful that I don't lock you in a cell next to Zeke."

"You wouldn't." She paled. He'd struck a chord.

"There are rules in life. You seem to take pleasure in flouting them, regardless of your situation."

"Most people would call that being independent."

"I call it stupid."

She let out a long breath, but no retort was forthcoming. Finally she asked, "What do I have to do?"

"Be pleasant and respectful. Is that so hard?"

"No."

"If Mom agrees, you can stay here until the hearing. I strongly suggest you find someone to make your bail."

"Fine," she mumbled, and Wyatt felt a moment of sympathy for her.

On the surface, she seemed to have everything, looks, intelligence and money. Yet he saw a lost little girl fighting for something. She probably didn't even know what that was. He certainly didn't.

He entertained the idea of letting her go on her own recognizance. But there was something about justice. Right and wrong.

And there was something about Peyton Ross.

THEY WALKED into the kitchen as Mae was getting food out of refrigerator for lunch.

Peyton looked at Wyatt and cleared her throat. "Mrs. Carson, I'm sorry I complained about the dishes."

"Sure, hon." Mae placed a loaf of bread on the table. "We may not have a fancy dishwasher, but we all help out around here. Don't we, Jody?"

"Yep."

"So if you'll put ice in the glasses and pour the tea, we'll forget about the little incident."

"Thank you." Peyton went to the refrigerator, not even looking for an icemaker. She knew there wasn't one. Finding ice trays, she pulled them out and popped ice into the glasses on the counter.

"You have to refill them," Jody said, pointing to the trays.

Great. Now she had three people telling her what to do. But she did the chore without frowning or cursing. That was an accomplishment.

"I'm getting paper plates." Jody ran to a pantry. "I don't like doing dishes, either." She plopped paper plates and napkins on the table. "Grandma, when are we getting a dishwasher?"

Wyatt stroked his daughter's hair. "Grandma likes her house the way it is, Jody. Let's have lunch."

Peyton dutifully poured the tea and took her seat. Nothing much was said as they made ham-and-cheese sandwiches with lettuce, tomatoes and pickles.

Afterward, Peyton picked up the plates and threw them into the garbage. She carried the glasses and the silverware to the sink. Staring at the dishes, she wondered what to do next. Water, of course. She wasn't an idiot.

A tangy male scent reached her a moment before Wyatt shoved a stopper into the drain. He turned a faucet and water spurted out. Opening a cabinet door beneath, he grabbed dish soap and squirted it into the water.

"Simple," he said, his eyes holding hers. For the first time she noticed the green highlights in the brown orbs. Very sexy. And warm. She felt it all the way to her painted toenails.

She drew herself up quickly, reached for a sponge and began to wash the dishes. There weren't many, and before long she had them perfectly aligned in the drainer to dry. She then released the water and wiped the sink and counter. Squeezing the sponge clean, she placed it on the sink. No problem. She'd washed dishes—the hard way. Maybe she could put that on a résumé.

"I need to talk to everyone before I go back to the office," Wyatt said.

"Okay, Daddy. What's up?" Jody stood in front of him, shifting from one foot to the other.

Wyatt looked down at his daughter. "Ms. Ross's brother is not able to get here, so she'll be staying with us until Wednesday."

"Where's she gonna sleep?" Jody asked.

Wyatt knelt down to be on Jody's level. "Since you have a trundle bed, I was hoping you'd let her sleep in your room."

"No way." Jody shook her head. "She snores."

Peyton wanted to dispute that, but decided to button her lip as suggested.

"You can sleep with me," Mae said to Jody. "We've done it before when we've had company."

"No way, Grandma. The last time I had to get up to go to the bathroom and bumped into your big Elvis. He started singing 'hunka hunka of burning love' and it scared me. I almost peed in my pajamas. I'm staying in my room."

Wyatt took Jody's arm and led her out onto the back porch.

"I can sleep on the sofa," Peyton told Mae.

"Let Wyatt handle it. He has a way with her." Mae placed a

plate of cookies on the table. "How about a chocolate-chip cookie? If worse comes to worst, you can sleep with me."

"I think a big Elvis might scare me, too."

"Oh, hon, you might be all shook up, but Elvis doesn't scare anybody." She waved a hand toward the refrigerator. "Bring the milk and glasses."

Peyton started to tell her she'd just washed the glasses and wasn't dirtying them again, but she wanted cookies, too.

As she ate her fill, she could see Wyatt and Jody sitting on the steps. She wondered what he was saying.

"Ms. ROSS DOESN'T snore, does she?"

"Yep, she does." Jody bobbed her head like a cork.

"She doesn't seem like a woman who snores."

"Not a real snore, but grunting noises, and they would wake me."

"Thunder doesn't wake you."

Jody rubbed Do's head. "I just don't like her."

"You said you'd help me," Wyatt reminded her, knowing he had to do a little scheming to convince her. He wouldn't force her, though.

"I'm being nice."

"I appreciate that." He hugged her. "But since Lamar was injured in the jailbreak, I'm short a deputy. I need someone to keep an eye on Ms. Ross. Do you think you could be my deputy for a couple of days?"

"Oh, boy." Her eyes went wide. "I can do it, Daddy. I can watch Ms. Ross."

"She'd have to sleep in your room."

"'Kay."

"But she snores."

"A deputy would do it, right, Daddy?"

"Right."

Jody clapped her hands. "Oh, boy! I get to be a deputy! I'm gonna tell Ms. Ross that she has to do what I tell her."

"Whoa." Wyatt caught her as she jumped up and he pulled her back down. "We have to talk about the rules."

"What rules?"

He held up a finger. "Rule number one—a deputy upholds the law. Number two—he makes sure his prisoners are comfortable and well taken care of, despite his own personal views. Number three—he never, ever, uses his position for gain or spite."

Jody's face pinched into a frown. "That doesn't sound like fun."

"I need your help, sunshine."

"'Kay. I'll be the best deputy ever and I won't be bossy like Grandma is sometimes."

"Well, we'll keep that to ourselves." He stood and took her hand. "This afternoon I want you to make Ms. Ross comfortable in your room and see to her needs. We have to take care of our prisoners."

"Yuck! That sounds like a maid."

"But the pay is very good."

"Oh." Her eyes brightened. "What is it?"

"Unlimited hugs and kisses from the sheriff."

Jody's cherub face split into a grin. "You're working me, Daddy, like Virgil says a good quarter horse works a steer. The steer never knows what's happening to him. I've been steer-worked."

Sometimes Jody was too smart for her own good, but he knew she'd keep her word. *How* she did it would be a whole different story, though.

As they started inside, Jody stopped. "Oh, you forgot. You have to deputize me." She held up her right hand.

Wyatt tried very hard not to smile. "Do you swear to uphold the law of Horseshoe, Texas, no matter what?"

"Yes, sir, I do. And Dolittle will help."

Now all Wyatt had to do was explain this to Ms. Ross.

A few minutes later he was standing with her on the back porch. After he told her, her eyes narrowed to tiny slits.

"You're kidding, right?"

"No. I'm just trying to find a solution to this situation and I'd appreciate your help."

"Oh, please." She flung back her hair. "You can use those tactics on your daughter, but they won't work on me. A child for a deputy? That's the height of lunacy. I will not be bossed around by a little kid."

"You're the adult. Work it to your advantage." He shrugged. "It's that or the jail. Your choice."

"You bastard. I am going to s—"

He placed a finger over her lips. "Save it for the judge."

Her eyes threatening, she bit his finger. Not hard, but enough to hurt.

He jerked away and sucked the finger, and then wished he hadn't. Chocolate, milk and Ms. Ross lingered on his senses. Damn it!

Swinging around, he headed for his car, leaving Ms. Ross to decide what she wanted to do. Either way he was tired of finding solutions while she continued to throw up roadblocks.

PEYTON STORMED into the house and went straight to the sofa where she'd left her cell. She called Quinn. It went to voice mail. Gripping the phone until her knuckles hurt, she fought tears. She wouldn't cry. The sheriff wouldn't make her cry.

She stretched out on the sofa. Her body ached. She wanted to go home badly. Pulling the phone to her, she poked out her aunt's number—the aunt whose husband was a Methodist minister. Before it could ring, she clicked off and closed her eyes, fighting more tears.

"Are you sleeping?" Jody asked.

Peyton opened one eye. "No."

"Grandma's taking a nap. I don't take naps."

"Go away."

"I can't. I'm on duty."

Peyton groaned and flipped over to lie facedown on the sofa.

"I pulled out the trundle bed, but you have to help me with the sheets. I can't do it by myself."

Peyton flipped back. "So you're letting me sleep in your room?"

"Yep. A deputy does that. But you can't snore."

"And you can't tell me what to do."

"But I'm the deputy."

Peyton sat up. "You're a kid."

Jody's face fell and Peyton felt a moment of remorse. She'd hurt the girl's feelings. "Okay," she found herself saying and knew she'd lost every ounce of sense she'd ever possessed. "You're the deputy. I'm the prisoner. What's the plan?" She was such a sucker for a sad face.

Jody stood up straight, her eyes twinkling. "We fix your sleeping quarters."

She followed Jody down a hall, feeling better. Being a deputy was important to Jody, and Peyton wasn't taking that away from her. The reaction made Peyton feel good about herself, too. She didn't know a thing about kids, but hurting one wasn't in her plans. Hurting the sheriff might be at the top of her list, though.

As she entered Jody's room, she stopped short. It looked like a boy's room. The trundle bed was a dark walnut, as was the dresser. The walls were a dull beige. Pictures of horses hung on one wall, along with a bridle and a rope. A basketball, a soccer ball and a football were on the floor, as well as a bat, helmet and kneepads. On a shelf were some photos and artwork of Jody's. There was nothing, absolutely nothing, feminine in the room.

Peyton picked up a photo, one of Wyatt and the pretty blonde.

"That's my daddy and my mama," Jody told her.

"Where is your mama?" Peyton had to ask.

"She died."

"Oh. I'm sorry." She didn't expect that response and she didn't want to make Jody sad.

Jody shrugged. "It's okay. I was little, so I don't remember her much."

Questions crowded Peyton's throat, but she didn't voice them. It always made her sad when people asked about her father.

She stared closely at the photo. The couple was standing, their arms around each other, their cheeks pressed together as they smiled at the camera. They were happy and in love. It was evident on their faces.

Carefully, she placed the picture back on the shelf. She now knew why Wyatt lived with his mother. He needed help raising his daughter.

A single, handsome sheriff in a small town flashed through her mind. She could only imagine the women who threw themselves at him.

Luckily, she wasn't one of them.

Chapter Nine

Considering everything the afternoon went smoothly. Jody watched her like a hawk and at times Peyton found it quite amusing. At others, extremely annoying.

Mae awoke from her nap, and Elvis songs reverberated through the house. After listening to "Love Me Tender" for the fifth time she and Jody went outside to escape. It was a warm summer day. Peyton sat on the steps while Jody played with the dog.

Big live oaks shaded the backyard. Deep-red roses snaked heavily on a lattice trellis, their opened buds turned toward the sun in a gorgeous array of color. Pink crepe myrtles nestled against the white frame house, along with more rosebushes. The wind gently moved an old wooden swing under the trees, and a hammock hung between two others. It was peaceful. Quiet. Well, almost. She could hear a low hum of traffic in the background.

If she had her wallet, she could take off. The thought startled her. What would that accomplish? A warrant would be issued for her arrest and then she would become a wanted criminal. She shuddered. Thank God, she had more sense than that.

Jody, tired of playing with Dolittle, took a break in the hammock. She maneuvered her way into it easily, but then the dog jumped on top of her and they both tumbled out.

Peyton was immediately on her feet to check whether Jody was hurt. But Jody rolled on the ground, laughing at the dog. Peyton relaxed, a strange feeling in her chest. Was this the way mothers felt when they thought their child was hurt? Ridiculous. She hardly knew the girl.

Dolittle barked at Jody and they rolled around on the grass. Jody seemed a bit lonely with only her dog for company. Peyton recognized the signs. She'd been lonely a lot in her life. Her mother worked long hours and Peyton rarely saw her. But she'd always had her father. He'd been there for her whenever she needed him. She wrapped her arms around her waist. She missed him so much.

"Jody!" Mae called from the door.

Jody leaped to her feet, brushing grass and dirt from her clothes. "Be right there, Grandma."

Peyton followed Jody indoors.

"I'm going to the diner to pick up supper," Mae said. A big purse dangled from her forearm, and her hair was combed into a mass of tight curls. Her lips were a bright pink. "Will you be okay while I'm gone?"

"Sure, Grandma. I'm on duty," Jody replied.

"Yes, well, whatever." Mae looked at Peyton. "Do you need anything, hon?"

A one-way ticket out of here. "Thank you, no," was all she said.

"'Come What May.'" Mae headed for a door off the kitchen, which Peyton saw opened into a utility room and then the garage. In a few minutes they heard an engine rev.

Peyton suddenly felt very tired. She went into the living room and sat on the sofa. Jody was a step behind her, as was Dolittle.

Mae hadn't cooked since Peyton had been here and she thought that strange. Answering everyone with Elvis song titles was weird, too. Mae seemed a tad out of touch.

"Does your grandmother ever cook?"

Jody shook her head. "No, she always gets food from the diner for supper. It's open most of the time. But she doesn't want Daddy to know."

"Why?" He was a police officer. Surely he had figured out what his mother was doing.

Jody shrugged. "Don't know. We just let Daddy think Grandma cooked it."

"Is your grandma a bad cook?"

"Yes. One time when there was a snowstorm and the diner was closed, Grandma made spaghetti. It was like glue. Even Do wouldn't touch it. The diner has good food, so I don't complain. Neither does Daddy."

Everyone in this town was weird! Peyton couldn't figure out any of them. How bizarre that Mae couldn't cook and wanted it kept a secret from her son.

Peyton curled up. "I'm taking a nap."

"'Kay."

She fell into a deep sleep, and but one invaded by troubled dreams. She was running through the woods and Zeke was chasing her with a gun. A shot fired and she froze. Was she hit? Instantly she was awake and sitting bolt upright, looking for blood on her body, waiting for the pain. The dream was that real.

She sucked in a deep breath and relaxed. Jody sat cross-legged on the rug watching her, rubbing Dolittle's head.

"You were making really strange noises," Jody informed her.

"Go away." Peyton ran her hands through her tangled hair, realizing her mosquito bites were stinging. Getting up, she walked into the bathroom for more ointment. Jody had followed and stood in the bathroom doorway.

Peyton turned from the medicine cabinet. "You don't have to follow me everywhere."

"Yes, I do. I'm on duty."

"Take a break." Peyton closed the door on her and sank to the floor. After a second she felt bad about her rudeness and opened it. Jody was still standing there, as Peyton knew she would be.

She applied the ointment to her bites.

"I'll do that," Jody said. "I'm supposed to take care of you."

A sharp retort sprang to Peyton's lips. She squelched it. Without a word, Peyton handed her the tube. Jody meticulously applied it to every bite.

"Thank you," Peyton said at Jody's expectant look.

"That's my job. I'm the deputy. You're the prisoner."

The prisoner. Peyton had a hard time seeing herself in that light. But that was exactly what she was.

Jody sat back on her heels. "What's your first name?"

"Peyton."

Jody made a face. "That's weird."

"It's my mother's last name."

"Oh," Jody replied as if that made sense. Then she asked, "How did you break the law, anyway? Daddy never told me your crime."

Peyton chewed on the inside of her lip, wondering how to tell an eight-year-old what she'd done. It was becoming a source of embarrassment for her. At the time, getting to a party was more important. Nothing mattered, but her needs. Had she always been like that? Sadly, she had to admit, she had. Her father had granted her every wish, and she expected the rest of the world to do the same.

Sheriff Carson showed her otherwise.

She swallowed. "Your father stopped me for speeding and I tried to bribe him to let me go."

Jody eyes opened wide. "You mean, with money?"

It took a moment for the truth to squeak out. "Yes."

"That was stupid. Nobody bribes my daddy."

Peyton pushed to her feet. "Yes, it was a stupid thing to do." She saw her dirty clothes still on the floor and realized she should find a way to wash them. She would need clean clothes for tomorrow. Picking them up, she asked, "Do you know how to wash clothes?"

Jody stood. "You look at the label and follow instructions. Grandma will help." A door slammed. "Grandma's back!" Jody shouted and ran to the kitchen.

When Peyton reached them, Mae was taking food out of a bag.

"Meat loaf, mashed potatoes, green beans, hot rolls and apple cobbler. How does that sound?" Mae asked.

"Yummy," Jody replied.

"Get the bowls," Mae said. "You know what we have to do."

In a matter of minutes Mae had everything transferred to her own dishes and warming in the oven. The diner's containers were stuffed into the bag and taken to the trash in the garage.

Peyton was mystified. "Do you really think you're fooling your son?"

Mae slipped on an apron. "I fooled my husband for years, or at least he let me think I did. He and my son have enough sense not to rock the boat. They like to eat."

"But why the deception?"

Mae's expression changed to one of pain, suffering and heartache. Peyton wished she'd kept silent. "I'm sorry. It's none of my business."

Mae quickly tied the apron. "Jody, go check and make sure the lid is on the trash can."

"'Kay, Grandma, but I know I closed it."

As Jody left, Mae turned to Peyton. "You're right. It's none of your business, but since you're staying with us, I'll tell you." She drew a breath. "When I lost my son, I lost interest in a lot of things. Cooking was one of them." She took another breath. "I know you think I'm a nutcase…."

"No, Mae, please. I'm sorry. I should never have said anything." Peyton felt so bad she wanted to cry. She had no right to question this woman's life. Or anyone's.

Jody rushed in. "All done."

Mae handed her a plastic-foam container from the diner. "Ginger sent this for Mrs. Wilcott. Please take it to her."

"'Kay."

Jody carefully took the plate and headed for the door. Suddenly she stopped. "Grandma, I can't leave my prisoner."

"I'll watch her."

"'Kay. She's not much trouble. I'll be right back, if Mrs. Wilcott doesn't talk my ear off."

When Jody was gone, Peyton apologized again. "I really am sorry. I didn't—"

"Don't worry about it." Mae took a seat. "No one ever mentions my firstborn. They think I'll have another nervous breakdown."

Peyton also sat at the table. She could tell Mae she'd also lost someone she'd loved very deeply and knew how she felt. But then she recalled how, after her father's death, it had always bothered her when people started sharing their own loss of a loved one, as if she could equate her misery with theirs. At the time, she didn't want to hear about anyone else's pain. Probably Mae didn't, either.

When Mae didn't say anything else, Peyton tentatively asked, "How long has it been?"

Mae rubbed circles on the tabletop with her forefinger. "Forty years."

"Oh." That shook Peyton. Did grief last that long?

"He was five years old and contracted meningitis." Mae

studied the motion she was making with her finger. "In a few weeks he was gone and it was the deepest pain I've ever endured. It was like someone had turned out the light in my world and I didn't want to live anymore. My husband didn't know what to do. Neither of us knew how to live without Johnny." She clasped her hands. "Then one day I heard an Elvis song and I started to awaken from my malaise. I could actually feel joy. I listened to another and another. Yes, I'm besotted with Elvis, but it gets me through a lot of bad days."

Peyton placed her hand over Mae's. She didn't say a word. She didn't have to.

"I joined the living again and I had Wyatt." Mae brushed away a tear. "I shouldn't be telling a perfect stranger all this. I don't even talk about it with Gladys, but…but today is Johnny's birthday. He's been strongly on my mind."

"Oh, Mae. May I call you Mae?"

"Of course."

"This has to be a rough day. I'm so sorry you had to put up with my insolence."

"We did bump heads. It actually pulled me out of the doldrums."

Peyton smiled, glad to be of assistance. "Did you start sneaking food in after that?"

"Yes. I was never any good at cooking, anyway, so I just brought food home from the diner and put it in my dishes. No one knew or said a word. It's become a town secret, and neither Ginger nor her mother has breathed a word. It's a Carson tradition." Her mouth twitched almost into a smile.

Peyton patted Mae's hands. "Whatever works."

There was silence for a moment. Peyton wanted to do something to get Mae's mind off Johnny.

"Mae, would you please help me with something?"

"If I can."

"Will you show me how to wash my clothes? I'll need something clean for tomorrow."

"You bet. Go get 'em and we'll throw 'em in the washer."

For the next few minutes, Mae showed her how to use the machine. Her top had to be hand washed, as did her bra, and laid on a towel to dry. Mae threw other clothes in with Peyton's capris to make a load. Mae paused when she picked up Peyton's thong.

"What in the world?"

"They're panties," Peyton explained.

"Lawdy. 'Lawdy, Miss Clawdy.' What you young girls wear these days. If I got that stuck in my crack, it'd take me a week to get it out."

Peyton burst out laughing and Mae joined her. And without a doubt Peyton knew she'd made a friend.

Mae added more clothes, including Wyatt's briefs. There was something about their undies tumbling together that seemed indecent. Yet…delightful.

Jody came racing back and they set the table for supper. Minutes later Wyatt strolled in and placed his Stetson on a rack by the door.

Jody leaped into his arms. "The prisoner is doing fine," she told him.

His eyes met Peyton's. She couldn't look away and she wondered why. She was mad at him, but in this warm house filled with love and heartache, she'd forgotten why she was upset with him.

Jody slid to her feet.

"Have you heard from your brother?" Wyatt asked.

In a heart-stopping second, it all came back. "No." She could see he wanted her out of his house, and that hurt. Again, she had to wonder why.

Chapter Ten

After supper, Wyatt took a shower and changed clothes. Since he was short a deputy, he was going back to work. Peyton wondered how he kept going. He hadn't had any sleep. But as a lawman, he was probably used to the long hours.

She, Mae and Jody watched *Kid Galahad* on video. Peyton wasn't familiar with any of the actors except Elvis. His movies had all been made before her time, but Mae was enthralled and the music was good.

Later, she and Jody took baths and went to bed. They left Mae watching *Roustabout*.

After her bath, Peyton did her nightly ritual of applying lotion to her face, arms and legs.

"Why do you put that stuff on?" Jody asked, running into the room from her bath, her pajamas hanging on her thin body.

Peyton was getting a little tired of the questions. But it made her think. Why *did* she do this every night? The cream on her face was supposed to keep her skin young. At twenty-eight how old could she look? Well, she was sure she had aged in the past few days and she had to keep those wrinkles at bay.

"For protection," she replied, smoothing lotion on her legs.

"From what?"

"Age."

"Are you old?"

"Ancient." She hid a smile.

Jody sniffed. "That stinks."

"I'll have you know this is Gardenia Blush." She took a whiff from the bottle. "Heavenly. Makes me think of moonlight, the South and a tall, hands—" Peyton stopped when she realized she was talking to a child.

"You're weird as Grandma."

Peyton put her cell phone on charge to avoid disputing that one. She didn't want to miss a call.

With hands on her hips, Jody pointed to the bottom bed. "That's where you sleep."

"I know," Peyton replied, bending down and crawling beneath the sheet. She wore her usual sleeping attire: cotton shorts and a matching tank top. Luckily she had that with her. She'd been planning to spend the night in Dallas.

Jody flipped off the light and hopped onto the top bed. "I sleep here. Dolittle does, too." There was quiet for a moment and then Jody added, "I still don't like you."

Peyton lay on her back, staring into the darkness. The girl's admission bothered her. Maybe she was a little spoiled and self-centered. Still... "Why?"

"You called me a girl and a brat."

Peyton turned onto her side, facing Jody's direction. "You do realize that you are a girl, don't you?"

"I'm Jody."

"Mmm." Jody seemed to have a real problem with her gender, and Peyton didn't have the skills to help her. She wanted to, though. What would make Jody deny she was a girl? Peyton suspected it had something to do with her father.

"I apologize for calling you a brat."

"Thank you, and I apologize for saying you snore. Daddy couldn't believe it."

She jerked her head up. "You told your daddy I snore?"

"Yep. He said you didn't seem like a woman who snores."

Well, well, the sheriff had paid her a compliment. She was curious. "Did he say anything else?" she asked, feeling as if she was in junior high.

"Just that you'd been through a bad time with Zeke and needed our help."

So he was remorseful over what had happened. Somehow that made her feel better. Flipping onto her back, she said, "Good night, Jody."

"'Night."

Dolittle barked.

"'Night, Do," Jody murmured.

"'Night, Do." Finding herself parroting Jody, Peyton almost burst out laughing. What was happening to her?

The night took hold, but sleep evaded Peyton. Everything was so quiet. Horseshoe, Texas, must roll up the sidewalks at night. There wasn't a sound anywhere except for the hum of the TV in the other room. So different from Austin, where something was always happening and the lure of the night, especially the clubs, had a pull like no other.

If her trip had gone according to plan, she would be partying the night away with her friends. *Her friends.* For the first time she thought of them. Not Giselle, Mindy or Bree had called or text-messaged. Why weren't they anxious about her no-show? Friends worried about friends, didn't they?

She curled up, feeling more alone than ever. The same way she'd felt since her father's death, but now the burden seemed heavier. Her father had cared about her welfare, and when she lost that security, she'd lost everything.

He'd been a history professor. Her mother complained a lot about him being lost in the past, but Peyton loved that about him. He was so intelligent, so cultured. In the summers she'd traveled with him abroad, and he would talk for hours about ancient ruins, ancient cultures. She'd listen attentively, but a part of her was more interested in the Italian hotties, the Greek tycoons or the French charmers.

Life was so different now. She was truly alone and unprepared for life without her father's protection and care. She was unprepared for real life. Hell, she'd never washed dishes or clothes. Pathetic for a woman her age. She was sure the sheriff would agree.

She hugged her pillow closer.

When are you going to take responsibility for your actions?

WYATT WALKED through the door at midnight, completely exhausted. Ms. Ross had turned his whole world upside down, and he wasn't going to get any rest until he saw the last of her.

The house was dark and quiet; even his mom had gone to bed. Today was Johnny's birthday and he hadn't even hugged her. It had been forty years, yet it was still a difficult day for her. Being a parent, he understood. Losing Lori had crippled him emotionally and if it hadn't been for Jody, he never would have survived. Sometimes it bothered him to admit that frailty. He was a man and supposed to be strong.

He wasn't, though. He was vulnerable. No one knew that but him.

He was hoping his mom would be up so they could talk. At supper, she seemed fine and he hoped she and Ms. Ross were getting along a little better. Two nights, one day and Ms. Ross would be gone—just a speck of time in the scheme of things.

No sweat.

Stopping outside Jody's door, he opened it slightly. From the moonlight creeping through the blinds, he could see his daughter sprawled every which way, but Ms. Ross lay curled in a fetal position, her blond hair splayed across her pillow. He felt a catch in his throat as he thought of Lori. So many times he'd seen her like that. Damn! Ms. Ross wasn't Lori.

He quietly closed the door and went to his room. He undressed and fell into an exhausted sleep.

THE NEXT MORNING Peyton awoke early needing to go to the bathroom. She slipped out, careful not to wake Jody. She hurried down the hall, her bare feet making no noise on the hardwood floor. Pushing open the bathroom door, she stopped short. Wyatt stood there, shaving, in his khaki slacks and bare feet, no shirt. All she saw was gorgeous, muscled male, fresh from the shower, drops of water still clinging to his wide shoulders. Her heart did a cha-cha right through her rib cage.

He turned to her, slanting his face to the right as he ran a razor down his cheek. "Oh, do you need the bathroom?"

A dusting of dark chest hair arrowed down his stomach and disappeared into his slacks. His tousled hair gave him a rakish, sexy look. Her abdomen tightened with sexual awareness, which she fought like hell. She couldn't be attracted to this man.

"Yes. I'd like to use the bathroom," she managed to say. "I'll come back."

"No need." He wiped the excessive shaving cream away with a towel and stepped out into the hall.

She scurried by him into the bathroom and closed the door. A lemony, soapy scent lingered, and Peyton had to catch her breath. Maybe she was still half-asleep. That was her only explanation. She *wasn't* attracted to the sheriff.

BREAKFAST WAS a rushed affair. Wyatt wolfed down cereal and left. After breakfast, Peyton's phone jangled and she made a dive for it. It had to be Quinn.

It was Giselle. "Peyton, what happened to you?"

She walked into the living room for privacy. "You're just now realizing I'm not there?"

"When you didn't show, I figured you decided to stay at the wedding."

"I didn't. I got arrested between Austin and Dallas."

"You're kidding. What for?"

"Remember those little tricks you talked about—flirting and bribery? Well, they don't work."

"You didn't." Laughter filled the phone.

"Yes, I did."

"Damn, Peyton, you know I'm always exaggerating."

"Yeah. I'll remember that in future."

"So did Quinn come to your rescue?"

Peyton sagged onto the sofa. "No, I'm still waiting."

"Are you in jail?"

"Sort of. On your way back to Austin, could you please stop in Horseshoe, Texas, and make my bail?"

"Peyton, I'm sorry. I met this cowboy-type stud whose father owns a gazillion-acre ranch. He's taking me there today and I'm not missing a second of time with this gorgeous hunk. You understand, right?"

"How about Mindy or Bree?"

"Bree hooked up with a Dallas Cowboy, and he had a friend who couldn't take his eyes off Mindy. I haven't heard from them since. They're not in our room and they don't answer their cells. I assume they're having one hell of a time."

"Yeah." *So much for friendship.* "Quinn will come. Have a great time."

Peyton stared at the phone and thought about her life, her friends. A moment of clarity blazed its way into her brain. Shopping marathons, traveling, clubbing, partying, drinking and an endless stream of guys she couldn't remember. It was all meaningless.

She tried so hard to fit in with her sorority sisters, but the honest truth was that a lot of their activities bothered her. She drank wine, but poured out the hard stuff when no one was looking. Lately she'd been drinking too much wine and she didn't like that about herself. Getting drunk made her ill the next day, so she started faking. She was good at faking. The girls bragged about their sexual exploits. Peyton had lied about taking guys home so her friends wouldn't tease her. Casual sex just wasn't for her. Bragging about things she hadn't done suddenly seemed juvenile.

Where did she go from here?

She heard voices in the kitchen. Maybe today she'd start to live her life differently. Maybe today she'd start to feel good about herself.

With a sigh, she joined Jody and Mae.

THE DAY PASSED quickly and Peyton never thought once about leaving. Tuesday was Mae's bowling day, so she was gone until midafternoon, leaving Peyton and Jody to entertain themselves.

After several tries, Peyton managed to get into the hammock. Jody slipped in beside her. The big live oaks shaded them and they fell asleep in the warmth of the summer day. Dolittle jumped on top of them and they both tumbled to the ground, laughing. Jody then chased Do until she was out of breath.

Mae returned with a watermelon and they cut it on the picnic table in the backyard. It was delicious and she spit seeds on the ground just like Jody. She was relaxed and at peace. She hadn't felt that way in a long time.

A jangling noise irritated her at first, then she realized what it was. Her cell phone! She fished it out of her pocket and saw it was Quinn. About time! She got up from the table and moved a few feet away.

"Where have you been?" she asked her brother without preamble.

"I'm sorry, Peyton. I got hung up."

"This had better be good, because I'm ready to strangle you. How could you leave me in jail?"

"How could you get arrested?" Quinn fired back.

She took a deep breath. "Okay, what happened?"

There was a long pause before he said, "Deidre came to the wedding."

"That bitch." Peyton was livid. Deidre Pennington had been stringing her brother along for years.

"I invited her, so you have no reason to be outraged."

"Oh, I'm only getting started, brother dear. She ditched you for another guy. Have you forgotten that?"

"Just listen to me, please."

She dragged in another breath. "I'm listening."

"Deidre's father has a new cabin cruiser on Lake Austin and she wanted me to see it. I agreed, but I planned to make it to Horseshoe, Texas, too, which is where you are, in case you haven't figured it out yet."

"This is Tuesday, you idiot. Of course, I've figured it out."

"Calm down."

"Just tell me what happened."

"Well, we had champagne at the wedding and we had more on the boat. The next thing I knew it was morning."

She gripped the phone. "Didn't you check your messages?"

"I left my phone in the car. I didn't want to be disturbed. And before you start yelling, I deserve some time off. I took the week because I was hoping Deidre and I could work out our problems. I didn't plan on you getting arrested."

"It didn't seem to make a difference."

She heard a long sigh. "Things just happened, okay? We'd taken the boat out and in the morning we couldn't start it. It drifted into a cove and another boater found us this morning and took us to my car. My phone was dead, but I got your messages at my apartment. I immediately called the governor's office, and I should be able to get all the charges dropped. I just got off the phone with the sheriff and he said the hearing is at ten tomorrow. I'll be on my way as soon as I hear from the governor's office."

"You talked to the sheriff?"

"Yes. He seems like a decent fellow. He mentioned something about a jailbreak. I'll sort it out as soon as I get there."

"You might as well wait until the morning because I'd have to come back for the hearing, anyway." What was she saying?

"You want to spend another night in jail?"

Peyton looked at Jody and Mae, who were staring at her with rounded eyes. "I'm not in jail. I'm staying with the sheriff's family."

"The sheriff you bribed?"

"Yes."

"Well, the good sheriff failed to mention that. I see a whole lot of loopholes in your case. But we won't worry about that, since we're getting the charges dropped. At least now I don't feel so bad—you're not in jail."

"Oh, brother dear, your pain hasn't even begun."

She clicked off before he could say another word.

Jody gazed up at her. "Was that your brother?"

"Yes."

"You yelled at him."

"Jody," Mae called. "Take this half of the watermelon to the refrigerator."

"'kay, Grandma." Jody darted away and Peyton thought how willing she was to do anything her grandmother asked of her. That was surely a lesson Peyton needed to learn.

PEYTON AND JODY set the table while Mae rushed to the diner. They finished putting out the food just as Wyatt walked in. As he placed his hat on the rack, she thought he looked tired. He was probably running on empty.

Jody dominated the conversation, so Peyton didn't get a chance to say her brother had called. When they'd finished eating, Peyton carried dishes to the sink and Wyatt followed. She put in the stopper and turned on the faucet.

Leaning against the cabinet, he said, "I guess you heard from your brother." So. He already knew.

"Yes."

"He told me he was unavoidably detained."

She attacked a plate with the sponge. "Yes, by an ex-girlfriend."

Wyatt didn't respond to the bite in her voice. "Tomorrow this will be over."

She wondered what was going to happen tomorrow. She'd tossed out so many threats, but a fraction of fear had her asking, "What's going to happen at the hearing?"

"Your brother, the sharp attorney, the one who is going to sue my ass, will have you back in Austin in no time."

"I'm not going to sue you or the town." She had intended to make this man hurt, but living in his house and spending time with his family, she'd lost that desire. And somewhere along the way she'd realized that a lot of what happened had been her fault.

"My department screwed up, so I appreciate that."

She set a plate in the drainer, focusing on what he'd said earlier. "So you think the charges will be dropped?"

When he didn't say anything, she glanced sideways at him. Deep grooves marred his forehead. She studied the intense expression on his chiseled face.

"You think the charges shouldn't be dropped, don't you?"

He took a glass from her and placed it in the drainer. "Let's just say justice will take a back seat tomorrow, so just accept the gift you've been given. And please don't *ever* try to bribe a police officer again.

"Jody," he called, turning away.

Jody and Mae were watching *Wheel of Fortune* in the living room. Jody screeched to a halt in front of her father. "You're going to work, Daddy?"

Wyatt lifted her into his arms. "Yes. I'll be home at midnight."

"Don't worry, Daddy. I'm on duty here."

Glancing at Peyton over Jody's shoulder, he replied, "I won't, sunshine." He kissed her cheek and Jody hurried back to the TV.

Wyatt reached for his hat, but he hesitated at the door. "I'm sorry you had a bad experience in my town."

Peyton rested against the cabinet and folded her arms. "Is that an apology?"

As he settled his hat on his head, his mouth curved into the closest thing to a smile she'd seen on him. "Don't push your luck. Just don't be so impulsive. Next time the lawman might not be so nice."

"Yeah, right." She couldn't stop the smile that played with her lips. But it ended quickly as he walked out of the room.

She tightened her arms around her waist. After tomorrow,

she'd never see Wyatt Carson again. Yesterday she'd been dying to leave his town.

So why wasn't she jumping for joy?

Chapter Eleven

"Are you going home tomorrow?" Jody asked as they pulled out the trundle bed.

"I have my hearing in front of a judge in the morning, and yes, I'm hoping to go home afterward." Peyton threw back the sheet and slipped into the bed.

Jody flipped off the light and then climbed into the higher bed. "Where do you live?"

"Austin."

"My mommy and daddy used to live there."

"Oh." Peyton hadn't realized that.

"My mommy died there and so Daddy brought me here to Horseshoe."

Peyton didn't know what to say, but obviously Jody wanted to talk. "How old were you?"

"I don't know."

The hint of sadness in the small voice was probably shadowed by things she didn't understand. Once again Peyton thought about bringing up the gender issue, but it was none of her business. After tomorrow, she'd be gone, and Jody would be only a fond memory. She was surprised that she wanted Jody to remember her the same way.

"I hate to leave with you disliking me," she said.

"I guess you're not so bad. Dolittle likes you."

The dog barked.

"'Night, Peyton," Jody said.

Peyton swallowed. "'Night, Jody. And Dolittle."

At the mention of his name the dog barked again.

"Shh," Jody scolded him. "You'll wake Grandma."

"I think Grandma's in Elvisland and unreachable." Peyton snuggled into her pillow.

"Yeah," Jody murmured sleepily. "She goes there a lot."

It was the only way the woman could deal with her grief. Peyton understood that completely. She, on the other hand, had been dealing with hers by destructive behavior. The thought was not comforting.

She tossed and turned, unable to sleep. Deciding she wanted a glass of milk, she got up and tiptoed out of the room. Dolittle whined, but didn't bark. Jody didn't stir.

On her way to the kitchen, she heard the TV click off, so she went into the living room. Mae sat in her recliner in her nightgown, an empty bowl of popcorn on her lap. "Oh, hon, do you need anything?" she asked when she saw Peyton.

She eased down on the rug in front of Mae. "No. I'm just a little nervous about tomorrow."

"That's the Way It Is," Mae answered with the title of an Elvis album, and then added, "Don't fret about it. I'm sure it will turn out fine."

Peyton didn't want to say that Mae's son would have her jailed for months if it was left up to him. She glanced around the room at all the family photos. There were pictures of Wyatt from the day he was born and there were many of Wyatt, his wife and Jody. Peyton was curious about the pretty blonde.

"May I ask you a question?"

"Sure."

"What happened to Wyatt's wife?"

Mae shifted uncomfortably and Peyton saw that it wasn't an easy topic for her to discuss.

"That's okay," she said quickly. "I was just curious."

"Oh, hon, around here we never talk about Johnny or Lori, and maybe we should. Then maybe the pain wouldn't be so bad. But we Carsons have a hard time opening up."

"A lot of people are like that." Her father had been. He'd kept his feelings inside, much to the frustration of Peyton's mother.

"Lori was killed in the line of duty," Mae said unexpectedly.

"So she was a cop, too?"

"Yes. She and Wyatt were police officers in Austin. Wyatt had already made detective, and Lori was applying when she became pregnant." Mae settled back into her chair. "Those two were inseparable since first grade. In high school Lori's parents divorced and Wyatt was there for her. After that, their relationship became serious, and I worried, like all mothers, about an early pregnancy. But Wyatt and Lori were always very responsible and determined about their future in law enforcement."

Mae set her popcorn bowl on the floor. "But I do believe Jody was a surprise. I never saw two more excited people, though. Lori worked right up until Jody was born and then took three months off. I was there for the birth, but I came home soon after because I knew they wanted to take care of the baby themselves."

"It sounds as if they were very much in love."

"Oh, yes, and I'm afraid my son will never love again. He's the type of man who only loves once that deeply."

"Does he date?" Peyton wanted to snatch the question back, but Mae didn't seem to mind her nosiness.

"Not to my knowledge. Jody and his job are his life now."

Peyton drew a breath and dared to continue, needing to know. "Was Lori shot?"

"Oh, no. Lori was off duty, but there was a big wreck on the freeway and she was called in to help with the congested traffic. She was directing cars, trying to get them around the wreck as safely as she could when a teenager in a sports car got tired of the long wait. His girlfriend was waiting and he decided he had to go. He tore around the long line of cars on the wrong side. Lori held up her hand to stop him, but he…he hit her. He said he didn't see her, but she had on one of those colored police vests. She died instantly, they said."

Ohmygod! Ohmygod!

Peyton sat paralyzed by the severe pain of realization, of truth and destruction. She was just like that teenager, thinking only of herself and her need to get to Dallas. She had never even seen the woman she'd almost hit. She hadn't seen a lot of things.

But the sheriff had.

Her flagrant disregard of the law must have reminded him of how Lori had died. Under the circumstances he was very cordial to her—because he was a lawman and respected the law.

She swallowed hard. "What happened to the teenager?"

"Never spent a day in jail." Mae clicked her tongue. "His family was wealthy and hired big-gun attorneys, as Wyatt called them, to get the kid free, and they did. He got a ten-year suspended sentence for involuntary manslaughter. The police community was not happy, so his dad moved him to California to continue his education."

Justice had taken another back seat. Money and power did that—just as it would tomorrow.

Peyton rose to her feet. "Thank you for telling me. I know it wasn't easy."

"I know you think my son is hard, but he's not. You just have to see him with Jody to know he isn't. You've realized that, haven't you?"

Peyton shoved her hands through her hair. "Yes, and now I understand why he's such a stickler for the law."

"He's always been that way."

"My brother is going to get my charges dropped." She wasn't sure why she was telling Mae that. Maybe she had to hear it out loud.

"I'm sure you'll do the right thing."

Peyton laughed nervously. "I'm not known for that."

"People change."

Did they? She really wanted to believe it was possible.

"I...I want to thank you for allowing me to stay here, especially with my attitude."

"You're welcome, hon."

Milk no longer interested her, so she turned toward Jody's room. Then she stopped. "Happy birthday to Johnny and may Elvis's music continue to bring you comfort."

Mae lifted an eyebrow. "So you don't think I'm a nutcase? That I live in 'Cotton Candy Land'?"

"No, far from it."

Mae pushed the handle on the recliner to a sitting position. "There's hope for you, Peyton Ross. 'Catchin' on Fast.'"

"Thank you." Peyton smiled at Mae's fetish for Elvis songs. With heavy feet, she made her way to her bed, but sleep was a gift for people at peace with themselves. She was far from feeling any peace with herself.

When are you going to take responsibility for your actions?

Maybe sooner than she'd ever imagined.

WYATT WAS OUT of the house before Peyton was awake. He didn't want to risk another encounter with her in the bathroom.

Peyton in short-shorts and a tank top had played hell with his morning. That wasn't going to happen again.

Today was the day.

Ms. Ross was leaving his jurisdiction.

He told his mom to give Jody a kiss for him. He never missed kissing her good morning, but with Ms. Ross in the house, things were different. At lunch, he'd give Jody tons of hugs and kisses. He'd be in a better mood, too.

Hardy Beckham, the district attorney, strolled into his office with his usual serious demeanor and a briefcase that always seemed attached to his hand.

"I want to go over the Ross case one more time." He eased into the chair across from Wyatt's desk, placing his briefcase at his feet.

Wyatt leaned back, the springs on his chair complaining, mostly from age, the chair's not his. "We've already discussed it, but I'm sure you've received a call from Quinn Ross."

"You bet, so we better have all out *i*'s dotted and our *t*'s crossed."

Hardy tended to get a little nervous when a high-powered attorney came to town. His father, Hardy Senior had been the D.A. for more than forty years. After a stroke, he'd retired. At his request Hardy Junior had returned from Houston to run for the position. Wyatt had seen Hardy many times in a courtroom and knew he had no reason to worry.

"From what I understand, the governor is sending a formal request for all charges to be dropped. Judge Fitzwater is not going to ignore that."

Hardy frowned. "So you're on board with this?"

Wyatt leaned forward and reached for his pen. Something about Ms. Ross getting off scot-free rubbed him the wrong way. Still…

"Zeke put her through a night of terror," he replied. "It was my department's fault he escaped, so I guess that balances out the charges."

Hardy eyed him. "I thought you'd fight this." Hardy was two years older than Wyatt and knew Lori's story and Wyatt's struggle to put her killer behind bars.

"Sometimes you have to let go."

"Tell that to someone who doesn't know you."

Wyatt stared back at his friend, not willing to discuss his leniency with Ms. Ross. "Let's stick to business."

"Okay. Ira signed off on admitting Zeke to a mental institution for evaluation. Once I told Zeke there were women there, he was ready to go. A van is arriving this morning to pick him up, and Thelma Boggs is following to make sure he gets settled into the place. We should have done this years ago."

"Yeah. I know the women of Horseshoe will be very grateful."

"I've pleaded out the Wilson brothers. They're doing six months' jail time."

"That should cause them to think about the error of their ways." Wyatt looked at his watch. "We better get over to the courthouse."

Hardy stood and reached for his briefcase. "What time are you bringing Ms. Ross?"

"Stuart is picking her up now."

"What do you mean Stuart's picking her up? Isn't she in jail?"

"No. She's staying at my mom's. I couldn't have her here with Zeke. That had already caused enough problems."

"Hmm." Hardy rubbed his jaw. "It's a good thing the charges are being dropped or we might have a problem."

"Listen, I did what I had to in order to keep her safe. If Ms. Ross's defense-attorney brother has a problem with his sister staying in a safe environment, then I say he's the one with the problem."

"I see," Hardy murmured in a tone that said he saw more than Wyatt wanted him to.

"You see nothing. Let's go."

PEYTON SAID her goodbyes to Jody and Mae and couldn't understand the lump clogging her throat. Lonely Jody insisting she wasn't a girl and Mae getting by on Elvis's songs. Two people and their weird ways had touched her deeply. Now it was time to go home.

The deputy drove her to the courthouse and said very little. She left her things in the patrol car and he escorted her inside the old courthouse. It smelled faintly of dust and mildew. Their footsteps echoed off the walls as they made their way to an ancient elevator. The courtroom was located on the second floor.

They walked down a hall where imposing pictures of former judges hung. Taking a left, they went through double doors to a small courtroom. Her eyes immediately found Wyatt standing with a man in a suit. They were talking with her brother. Finally, he was here.

Quinn noticed her and strolled to her side. He took in her appearance with one glance. "What happened to you?"

She wore her capris, sleeveless knit top and sandals. Self-consciously her hand went to her hair, which was combed. She didn't think she looked that bad.

"What do you mean?"

"You don't have on any makeup and there are red spots on your face and arms."

"Mosquito bites."

"Yes." His expression hardened. "I've just been hearing about everything that's happened to you and I'm out for blood. I don't care if the charges are being dropped. I'm going to do a number on this town, that sheriff and his department. If he can't protect his prisoners, how can he protect the citizens of this county?"

Quinn was saying everything she had told Wyatt he would. He would make Wyatt pay for everything that had happened to her. In the end, Quinn would make sure Wyatt lost his badge.

Just like she'd said.

Chapter Twelve

Before Quinn could vent any more, the bailiff announced that court was convening. They took their seats on the left side at a long oak table. On the right sat the man in the suit. Wyatt slid onto the bench behind him.

"All stand for the Honorable Judge Ira Fitzwater," the bailiff called.

Peyton stood beside Quinn, her mind buzzing. What was she going to do? This wasn't just about her. This involved other people's lives. Good people's lives.

"Be seated," the judge said.

Peyton's legs trembled and she was glad for the support of the chair.

I know you'll do the right thing.

When are you going to take responsibility for your actions?

Quinn pulled a folder from his briefcase with the governor's emblem on it. All she had to do was remain quiet and she could go home.

She glanced sideways at Wyatt, but he was staring straight ahead.

Tomorrow justice will take a back seat.

The same as when his wife had been killed.

"Your Honor, may I approach the bench?" Quinn requested.

The judge motioned him forward. Quinn picked up the folder and made his way to the judge's bench. This was it. Did she take responsibility for everything she'd done? Or did she let Quinn take care of her problems the way he always had?

For the first time in her life the latter was not acceptable. She stood on legs that still trembled. She gripped the table.

"Your Honor, may I say something, please?" came out in a voice similar to Daffy Duck's. She took a calming breath.

Quinn whirled around. "Sit down, Peyton. This will be over in a minute."

The brainless-child treatment hit her like scalding water. Her backbone stiffened and her jittery indecision vanished.

"I will not sit down. I have something to say."

"May I have a moment with my client, Your Honor?" Quinn asked.

"By all means." The judge sat back.

"No," she said with force. "I…I want to represent myself."

Quinn hurried to her side. "What the hell are you doing?"

"I wish to represent myself, Your Honor." This time she said it loudly and with confidence, ignoring Quinn's angry face.

"Have you lost your mind?" Quinn hissed.

"Are you sure, Ms. Ross?" the judge asked. "You're facing some serious charges."

"I know exactly what I'm facing."

Her past, so she could face her future with pride.

"Then, Mr. Ross, I don't believe your services are required."

"Your Honor, my sister has been through a horrendous ordeal due to the incompetence of the sheriff's department and I'm not sure she's in her right mind. I request a few minutes with her."

"Your Honor, I'd like to make a statement." Now that she'd made her decision, nothing was going to stop her.

"Peyton…"

She turned to her brother. "Go home, Quinn. I'm sorry I called for your help. I don't need it. This time I'm taking care of my own life."

"Go ahead, Ms. Ross," the judge instructed, keying something into the laptop on his right, which surprised Peyton. She didn't know this small town had Internet service.

She took a deep breath, her fingertips pressing against the hardened surface of the table. All she had to do was say the words. Clearing a lump that felt like a pinecone from her throat, she said, "I plead guilty to all the charges. I was speeding through Horseshoe without any regard for the safety of others."

"My God!" Quinn sank into his seat.

"I truly didn't hear the siren because I was wearing an earbud. When I did pull over, I was angry that the sheriff had stopped me. I was eager to get to a party in Dallas. When I saw he wasn't going to cooperate, I offered him a hundred dollars to let me go."

Quinn buried his face in his hands.

"Anything else, Ms. Ross?"

She swallowed the rest of the pinecone. "Yes. In the jail the man, Zeke, kept pestering me about marriage. I told him to leave me alone and that the only thing I wanted was to get out of jail. I didn't realize he had diminished mental capacity and I should have—it was very evident. He took my words to mean I'd marry him if he got me out of jail, which he did. I tried to get away once we were outside, but I couldn't. He was very strong. And—" she curled her hands into fists "—this isn't easy for me to admit, but if I had gotten away from him, I would have tried to make my way to Austin. The jailbreak was my fault and I don't hold anyone responsible but myself."

"What the hell is she doing?" Wyatt whispered to the D.A.,

but Peyton heard him clearly. "Do something. Get Ms. Ross out of my town."

"Ms. Ross, I don't believe anyone has ever been this honest in my courtroom," the judge said, ignoring the sheriff's muffled outburst.

"Or this insane," Quinn said.

The D.A. got to his feet and buttoned his jacket. "Your Honor, the state respectfully drops all charges against Ms. Ross."

The judge held up a hand. "Not so fast, Hardy. Ms. Ross is being honest and the court wants to honor that."

The D.A. glanced at Wyatt and back to the judge. "The state respects her honesty and apologizes for any hardships she endured while in our jail."

"Now, Hardy, you and Wyatt seem mighty eager to sweep a crime under the rug. I don't do good-ol'-boy tactics in my courtroom."

"Your Honor—"

"Sit down, Hardy."

The judge turned to Peyton. "I admire your honesty and your need to make things right. That takes character." He glanced at the paper file in front of him. "I'm throwing out the jailbreak incident. There's enough fault to go around on that one. But I don't take the bribery charge lightly, even though our esteemed district attorney seems to." He spared the D.A. a glance.

"I am sorry for what I did," Peyton said, "I'm ready to serve any sentence you think is fair."

The judge pondered the request and then scribbled something in the folder and keyed something into the laptop. "Three hundred hours of community service in Horseshoe, Texas. Maybe next time you'll think twice before trying to bribe an officer of the law."

Peyton shifted her weight to one foot. "I hate to sound dumb, but I'm not clear what community service means."

Quinn groaned.

"It means you will not spend any time in jail, but you will spend time helping the community in such things as picking up trash or aiding the elderly. The Meals on Wheels program needs volunteers. This will be done during the day, just like a job."

"Will I be able to go home on weekends?"

"No. Not until you've served your hours. At eight hours a day, five days a week, you'll be spending about two months with us. I'm hoping, Ms. Ross, that you'll gain a deeper respect for this community and for yourself."

Quinn stood. "Your Honor, could the sentence please be commuted to Austin?"

"No," the judge replied promptly. "Ms. Ross will work out her sentence in Horseshoe where the crime was committed. Sheriff Carson will oversee her duties and find her a place to live."

Wyatt was instantly on his feet. "Ira, that's not in my job description."

The judge looked up. "It is now."

Wyatt mumbled a curse word under his breath.

The judge looked over the rim of his glasses. "It's a good deal, Wyatt. Ms. Ross will learn to respect the law and you'll get across to your officers to be more cautious when dealing with wily prisoners like Zeke."

"May I have my car back, please?" Peyton asked.

"I'm not inclined to grant that, Ms. Ross. It might prove too much of a temptation." The judge banged his gavel. "This court is adjourned."

Wyatt grabbed his hat and stormed from the room.

Peyton stared after him. He was angry. She'd thought he'd be happy that she was finally taking responsibility for her actions.

She let out a long breath, grateful she didn't have to spend any time in jail, just in Horseshoe, Texas. Were they the same? She should have thought this through a little more. Picking up trash? What had she done?

The snap of Quinn's briefcase jolted her and she met her brother's furious gaze. "Have you completely lost your mind?"

She didn't bat an eye. "How many times in the past six months have you told me to grow up?"

"More than I can count," he admitted, his demeanor softening just a fraction.

"Well, today I grew up. Why aren't you happy?"

Deep grooves visited his forehead. "Do you know what Mom is going to say when she hears you're doing community service in Horseshoe backwater, Texas?"

"Mom doesn't consult me about her decisions, so I don't feel I need to consult her about mine."

He slipped his hands into the pockets of his tailored slacks. "Peyton, you're not doing this as a way to get back at Mom, are you?"

"No." She was surprised that she meant it. "This is about me, my life and my choices."

"Fine." He reached for his briefcase. "You're on your own, kiddo. After taking up the governor's time for nothing, I'm sure my name will be mud for a while. Don't call me for anything." He strolled toward the door and suddenly stopped. Pivoting, he walked back to her.

"You irritate the hell out of me, Peyton, and I say things I don't mean. Call if you need anything. You know I'm a sap where you're concerned."

She threw her arms around his neck and hugged him tightly. "I really don't know what I'm doing. All I know is that I have to start taking care of my own life, my own problems."

"You're not going to need me anymore, huh?"

She drew back and brushed away a tear. "Now you'll have more time for Deidre." She dragged out the name.

"I can see that makes you so happy."

"Mmm."

"Do you need money?"

She shook her head.

"Bye, sis. And good luck." He kissed her cheek and walked out the door.

All her indecision returned.

She wrapped her arms around her waist and prayed she was doing the right thing. She was known for her impulsiveness, but she'd never done anything like this before. Instead of going home to the comfort of everything that was familiar, she would now be spending at least two months in Horseshoe.

Picking up trash.

Maybe she *had* lost her mind.

"Ms. Ross."

She swung around to see the deputy standing there with her purse and suitcase.

"Thank you," she said, reaching for them. "Do you know where I go now?" She didn't have a clue and she hated to keep asking questions that probably were simple to everyone else.

"I'm on patrol, but I'll escort you to the sheriff's office."

"Oh. Thank you." But she wasn't quite sure she was ready to face Wyatt. He was so angry.

If he wanted to see justice served, then he had to be prepared for the consequences. Peyton Ross was spending more time in his town whether he liked it or not.

WYATT MARCHED into his office and threw his at the hat rack. It missed and landed on the floor. He ignored it and began pacing.

Crazy woman! Craziest woman he'd ever met in his life. What was she thinking?

Hardy walked in and took in Wyatt's agitated state. He sat down and propped his cowboy boots on Wyatt's desk. "Well, well, now isn't this a fine kettle of fish?"

"Shut up, Hardy." Wyatt picked up his hat and jammed it on the rack.

"You seem mighty upset for some reason."

"I'm not babysitting Ms. Ross. Ira can kiss my ass."

"Aren't you the same lawman who fought for two years to put Lori's killer behind bars?"

Wyatt sank into his chair, the knots in his stomach coiled so tightly it felt as if they'd snap.

"Wouldn't it have been nice if that kid had stood up in a courtroom and admitted his guilt, his negligence? Wouldn't it be refreshing if every criminal did that? I admire what Ms. Ross did today. That took guts, and I can't quite figure out where you're coming from. You've always been a straight shooter, justice first and always. Justice was done today, Wyatt."

"Yeah." The coils unwound slightly. "I never thought she'd do that."

"And…?"

Wyatt's eyes narrowed. "I've put up with her since Sunday and I was really looking forward to my life getting back to normal."

"You mean, back to boring."

Wyatt sighed. "Go to work, Hardy. I don't need your armchair psychology. And get your feet off my desk."

Hardy brought his feet to the floor. "When you're making out her list of duties, don't forget the courthouse. She sure could brighten up *my* day."

The door opened, preventing Wyatt from delivering a scathing remark. Ms. Ross stood there with her suitcase and purse in her hands, a hesitant expression on her face.

Was he never going to be free of this woman?

Chapter Thirteen

Hardy tipped his hat. "I look forward to seeing you around Horseshoe, Ms. Ross."

"Thank you," she replied.

Hardy had always been a sucker for a pretty face. Not Wyatt. But now he was stuck with the fancy, smart-mouth, incredibly beautiful woman. Three hundred hours would take roughly two months, but if he fudged, he could have her out of Horseshoe in six weeks.

First, he had to find a place for her to live for the duration. She certainly wasn't staying with them any longer. She'd disrupted his peace of mind enough. Not to mention raised his blood pressure.

He pointed to a chair. "Have a seat, please."

She sat on the edge of the chair Hardy had vacated, not saying a word. He found that a little odd. She was always talking.

Opening his address book, he searched for an understanding person who would offer accommodations to a stranger.

He picked up the phone and poked out a number. Mrs. Satterwhite answered on the first ring. She was a widow with a large house.

"This is Wyatt Carson," he said.

"Why hello, Sheriff."

"Mrs. Satterwhite, I have a small problem and I was hoping you could help." He looked at Ms. Ross and she gazed back at him.

"You know I will if I can."

"I'm looking for accommodations for a young woman for about two months."

"Are you talking about *that woman* who tried to bribe you and almost ran over poor Harriet? I just came from the beauty shop and I heard she's going to be staying in Horseshoe for a while. Ira must be getting senile."

Wyatt gritted his teeth. In Horseshoe gossip was faster than a speeding bullet. How the hell could news travel that fast?

"She'll be doing community service."

"I'm sorry, Sheriff. I can't have anyone like that in my house. I live alone and she might steal everything I have. I wouldn't be able to sleep a wink."

"I wouldn't want you to lose any sleep," he replied with as much calm as he could muster.

Next he tried Mrs. Hornsby, another widow.

As he waited, Peyton crossed her legs. Leaning over, she ran a hand down her shin, inspecting a mosquito bite. Inviting cleavage caught his eye, and every cell of his body came to full attention.

He glanced away as Mrs. Hornsby came on the line.

"Mrs. Hornsby, I was wondering if you had an extra room. I—"

"It's for *that woman,* isn't it?"

"If you mean Ms. Ross, yes."

"Now, Sheriff, you know I'm willing to help whenever I can, but I can't have *that woman* in my house."

"Judge Fitzwater wants her to stay in town and I don't think you'd have a problem."

"If Ira is so set on having her in Horseshoe, then let her stay with *his* family."

Damn it! The grapevine had already done its dirty work. No one was going to offer Ms. Ross a place to stay. But he didn't give up. There had to be someone who hadn't heard the news.

He dialed another number. No luck.

And another. No luck there, either.

Peyton ran her hands through her hair, the knit top showing off her full breasts. He slammed down the phone.

Suddenly Jody burst through the door, followed by his mom and Dolittle.

"Hey, Peyton, we heard!" Jody said, running around the desk and hopping onto Wyatt's lap. "Can I still be a deputy, Daddy? I'll watch her real good."

"Ms. Ross isn't under arrest anymore," he replied. "She'll be doing community service. I was just looking for a place where she could stay."

"Nonsense," Mae snorted. "She'll stay at our house. She already knows us."

"That's not a good idea." Wyatt tried to be as tactful as possible with Ms. Ross in the room.

"Why ever not?" Mae wanted to know.

"Because I have to supervise her duties and I don't want anything to cloud my judgment."

"Like what?"

"Mom!"

Peyton stood. "It's okay, Mae. It's probably better if I stay elsewhere."

"Hogwash. Get your things. My car is outside. Jody and I were on the way to the grocery store. You can came with us." His mother lifted an eyebrow at him. "Unless her duties start today."

"Whatever." He sighed deeply, knowing he was fighting a losing battle. "But first, I'd like a word with Ms. Ross."

"Sure. Let's go, Jody." Mae winked at Peyton. "I'm parked right outside."

"Daddy, does this mean Peyton'll have to sleep in my room again?"

"Looks like it." He waited for the refusal, but he waited in vain.

"Okay." She wagged her head. "But you need to start paying me to house prisoners. And I don't mean with kisses."

Wyatt felt like smiling for the first time today. As long as Jody was happy, nothing else mattered.

"How about a dollar a week?"

"Deal." She kissed his cheek, hopped off his lap and ran after her grandmother, Dolittle loping behind.

That left him alone with Ms. Ross.

He closed his address book, taking his time. He wasn't sure what to say to a woman who was like a thumbtack pressing on a nerve. But he knew he had to say something.

She spoke first. "I don't understand why you're so angry. You're the one who asked when I was going to take responsibility for my actions. It wasn't easy to do that and—"

"Why did you?" His eyes caught hers.

"Your mother told me about your wife and how the young driver went free. I saw myself so clearly in his actions, and I didn't want justice to take a back seat. I wanted—"

He quickly cut her off. "You know nothing about my wife." He didn't talk about Lori to anyone.

"I didn't say I did, and you can take that short-fuse temper and stuff it where the sun don't shine." She picked up her case. "Is there a motel in this town?"

"Out on the highway. The Do Drop Inn."

"That's where I'll be staying. You see, I have an aversion to staying in the same house with you, too." She whipped toward the door. "I'll be here at nine tomorrow morning."

"Make it eight."

She turned. "What?"

"Eight o'clock sharp. Is that a problem?"

"No."

He opened a drawer and pulled out her wallet. "You might need this."

She yanked the wallet from his hand, her eyes blazing. "So justice is something you spout, not something you practice?"

"Ms. Ross—"

"Go to hell." With that she made her exit.

He stood and stretched his tight muscles, feeling like a heel. It wasn't like him to be so cruel. *Don't Be Cruel.* Oh, God! The women in his life where driving him right around the bend.

Drawing a deep breath, he took a moment to regain his composure. He'd been preaching justice to Ms. Ross for days and he *was* impressed that she'd made a stand. So what was his problem?

His reaction to her.

After Lori, his interest in women had disappeared. That was fine with him. He had no desire to be with a woman; that part of him was dead.

He was lying to himself.

Ms. Ross stirred emotions in him he wanted to keep buried with Lori, the love of his life. Somehow Peyton Ross had tested that loyalty, tainted that love. It wasn't her fault, though, it was his.

Out the window, he could see her climb into his mom's car. He pulled out a calendar and marked a circle around tomorrow's date, the start of her community service. Two months. There was no doubt she'd survive it.

But would he?

PEYTON HAD a hard time talking Mae into dropping her at the motel. But she couldn't go back to the Carson house. She wasn't welcome there. Wyatt had made that very clear.

To say the Do Drop Inn was a dump was paying it a compliment. It was a row of about ten rooms with a small office. The army-green paint was peeling and several rusty screens lay on the cracked concrete. The Vacancy sign drooped sideways from a broken awning. The place looked like something out of an Alfred Hitchcock movie.

She started to beg Mae not to leave her, but pride, stubborn pride, made her get out of the car. Waving goodbye, she stepped into the dingy office and caught her breath at the stench of cigarette smoke.

A woman, who had to be at least eighty, sat behind the counter, a lit cigarette dangling from her lips.

"What you need?" the woman asked in a raspy vice.

"A…a room."

"The boyfriend outside?"

She took a breath, and then wished she hadn't. Her lungs filled with smoke.

"I don't have a boyfriend," she stated flatly.

"A pretty thing like you all alone? That doesn't make sense. Why do you want to stay *here*?"

Peyton decided she didn't need to answer that. "A room, please."

A few minutes later Peyton stood in a room that chilled her to the bone. The carpet was more like dirt and it was clear it hadn't been vacuumed in weeks, if ever. The stale smell of cigarette smoke and mildew was even worse. The bathroom was filthy. She quickly closed the door and stared at the stained bedspread.

She couldn't stay here. She couldn't even breathe without feeling nauseous.

A huge cockroach scuttled across the carpet, followed by another. This was probably a breeding ground for the critters. Panic seized her.

Just then a rat the size of a squirrel darted under the bathroom door. Peyton screamed and jumped onto the bed, removing a sandal. It was all she had to protect herself.

Panic nudged desperation and fear. What was she going to do? If this was growing up, then it sucked.

She could be in her tastefully decorated bedroom, soaking in her Jacuzzi, anything she wanted at her fingertips. But, oh, no, she had to do the right thing.

Grab your cell and call Quinn. That was all she had to do to make all her worries disappear. She'd be the cream puff she'd always thought she was. Her friends and family would agree. Her life was meaningless. *She* was meaningless. Admit it and get the hell out of this hick town.

But she didn't move.

In that moment she knew without a doubt that she had lost her mind—all because *his* opinion mattered.

"Go to hell, Wyatt Carson," she yelled at the rat, and then she burst into tears.

TOWARD THE MIDDLE of the afternoon, Wyatt's conscience ratcheted into overdrive. He wouldn't sentence anyone to that fleabag motel, so he couldn't leave Ms. Ross there and live with himself.

He drove to the motel and asked Mrs. Bagley her room number. Like everyone in Horseshoe, Mrs. Bagley was very curious.

"What'd she do, Sheriff? Is she that woman everyone is talking about?"

He ignored the question. "The room number, please?"

"Two."

A rat scurried across his boot and he cursed. "Mrs. Bagley, your son has been warned about getting this place up to code."

"That's Abner's business. I just watch the desk."

Smoke clogged his sinuses. "One month." He held up a finger. "If it's not up to code, the town will close it down and I'll be happy to carry out the order."

In response, Mrs. Bagley blew smoke rings into the air. Wyatt left.

He made his way to room number two and knocked. "Ms. Ross, it's the sheriff. Open up."

"I can't," came through the thin-paneled door.

"Why not?"

"Because…because…"

Wyatt tried the door and it opened. Ms. Ross stood in the center of the bed with a sandal in her hand and a look of panic on her face.

"What are you doing?"

"Defending myself from a giant rat."

"Let's go," he said.

"Where?" She had the audacity to question him.

"To my mom's."

"Why?"

"Ms. Ross, do we have to discuss this here?"

"I'm not going anywhere until you call me Peyton."

Was she kidding?

"Listen, do you want to leave this place or not? I'm not going to quibble with you."

"My name is Peyton," she stated, and slid a foot into the sandal.

The urge to turn and leave was strong, but if he did he knew his mother would never let him hear the last of it. And he wouldn't wish this place on his worst enemy.

"You're still in my custody." He stalled. For some reason he knew that the moment he called her by her first name, things would change between them. He'd rather keep the status quo.

"Bull."

"Damn it, woman. Get your ass in my car or I'm leaving you here." Turning, his long strides carried him to his vehicle.

She was at the passenger side before he could open his door. Hiding a smile, he slid into his seat.

"I'm not going to thank you," she said as he backed out, "because I know it wasn't your idea."

"Don't push your luck, Ms. Ross."

"Peyton," she said.

He glanced briefly at her and said what she wanted him to. "Peyton."

The name was a new sensation to his tongue, his senses. He wanted it to feel foreign and unfamiliar, but it felt good. It reminded him of chocolate-covered strawberries and champagne. Celebration. Seductive smiles. Long, lazy nights and tangled sheets…

He immediately rejected the images. But his body had already formed a welcome party. His heart never would, though.

His heart belonged to Lori.

Chapter Fourteen

The next few days were tense, to say the least. But Wyatt put his personal feelings aside and concentrated on his job as sheriff. Fitting Peyton into his schedule was a challenge.

He had no problem calling her by her first name now. He just wished it wasn't so...natural.

Since he was still short a deputy, he needed someone to sweep the office and clean the bathrooms.

When he told her her duties, she asked, "May I have rubber gloves, please?"

"They're in with the cleaning supplies in the back room."

At her puzzled look, he strolled to the room and opened a cabinet. "Supplies here." Swinging open a closet door, he added, "Broom and dustpan here. Any questions?"

"Well..."

"Don't ask me how to do it. Figure it out."

He waited for her to balk, but she didn't. In fact, she did exactly as she was told. Although her sweeping technique looked more like dancing and he had to look away. Crazy woman!

There were no prisoners, so that made things easier, except his mom had taken Peyton to the dollar store and she'd bought denim shorts and T-shirts. Peyton walking around his office in shorts wasn't doing his blood pressure any good.

The next day Wyatt got a call from Horace, the police chief of Bramble. There'd been a big fight at the local saloon and his jail was full. Four prisoners were transferred to Horseshoe.

At lunchtime he sent Peyton to the diner to pick up lunch for the prisoners. The next thing he knew all hell was breaking loose. The prisoners were whooping, hollering and whistling.

He jumped to his feet to see what was going on.

"Hey, Sheriff!" one prisoner shouted. "Horace didn't tell us you had Daisy Duke working for you. Hot damn, this is service!"

"Shut up and settle down," Wyatt said, taking Peyton's arm and pulling her into his office.

"They're just being guys," she said. "You know, idiots with too much testosterone."

He glanced at her and thought she was handling the situation surprisingly well. "It doesn't bother you when guys act like that?"

"Yes. But I don't think I have the power to change nature."

"Mmm." Wyatt took his seat as Stuart came into the office.

"All set," Stuart said.

"Stu's going to take you on a trash detail. It will be less stressful, and it's what the judge had suggested."

An hour later his phone started ringing off the hook. Wives were complaining. Their husbands were driving by just to watch Peyton pick up trash. They wanted him to do something with *that woman,* as Peyton was becoming known around town.

He called Stu and told him to take Peyton to his mom's. Her day was over. It was all he could take; the thumbtack was firmly embedded in his last nerve.

The next day he called Betty Tompkins, who was head of the Meals on Wheels program. She was eager for help, so Wyatt sent Peyton over, feeling this was foolproof.

He was wrong. By the end of the day his phone was ringing

again. Betty said Ms. Ross's help was causing problems. Perfectly healthy men were calling wanting meals brought to them. She had to let Ms. Ross go.

Wyatt was at his wit's end. He wasn't sure what to do with Peyton. But it was the weekend, so he thought he'd give it a rest until Monday. He wished Ira had allowed her to go home. It would have given them all a break.

And he needed a break.

On Saturday he stayed away from the house. He'd been doing a lot of that lately. It bothered him that Jody didn't seem to mind. That evening he was home in time to take everyone to the shindig on the courthouse lawn. Once a month the townspeople gathered to share their lives, their problems and good food. Wyatt always attended to make sure the event went off without incident. Jody and his mom loved it, too. Peyton went along and he was hoping there wouldn't be any trouble with the town's women.

He was braced for anything, though, especially with Peyton dressed in shorts and a T-shirt that had *Make My Day* written across the front.

Basically everyone left her alone. She sat by herself on a bench while women shot daggers at her with their eyes. Their better halves couldn't take their eyes off her. But no one socialized with her. Jody brought her a hot dog and introduced her to Virgil and Ramrod.

"This is Peyton," Jody said. "She's staying with us."

Ramrod took her hand and kissed her knuckles. "Just as pretty as a brand-new speckled pup in a shiny red wagon."

Virgil slapped Ramrod on the shoulder. "What kind of talk is that? Forgive my brother, ma'am. He's not much of a poet." He took Peyton's hand. "You're as breathtaking as a field of bluebonnets."

"Thank you, I think," Peyton said, glancing at Wyatt and noticing the way the women gravitated to him. He was talking to a brunette now.

Jody stared at the brothers. "What's wrong with you two? You're acting weird."

"Now, little bit, we're just being polite," Ramrod replied.

Peyton thought he was aptly named. Tall and beanpole thin, she wondered how he kept those faded jeans up. He didn't have hips or a butt. He was bald on top, but had gray hair around his ears, which he pulled back into a low ponytail.

Virgil was just the opposite, short and portly and completely bald.

Jody sat on the bench beside Peyton. "Virgil and Ramrod teach me a lot of stuff."

"Do they?" Peyton asked, wondering why Jody wasn't playing with the other kids.

"Yep." Jody bobbed her head. "Sleep with your boots on in bad weather. You never know when you might have to make a quick getaway. Always say you're sorry even if it tastes like a bull nettle in your mouth. And be polite even if it feels like sticking a needle in your eye."

Peyton took a bite of the hot dog. "I can truthfully say I've never heard that before."

"They have all kinds of sayings. When they were kids they had to walk ten miles in the snow to school uphill—both ways."

"Really." It rarely snowed in Texas. Uphill both ways? The two old geezers were pulling Jody's leg. And telling some mighty tall tales.

"We'll leave you two lovely ladies on that note." Ramrod bowed from the waist.

"They don't usually act like that," Jody informed her as they walked away. "You want popcorn? I'll get popcorn." In a flash she was gone.

Peyton watched everyone milling around, talking, laughing and sharing. She didn't miss the glances cast her way.

Right back at you, she wanted to say.

She finished off the hot dog and settled back. People were sprawled all over the lawn. A huge barbecue pit on wheels was parked to the side and a couple of men were making hot dogs and hamburgers. A popcorn machine and a cotton-candy maker were going full-tilt. There were also a group of women making ice cream. Watermelons were iced down in washtubs. A band was tuning up and the twang of a guitar echoed through the tall live oaks. Cotton Pickin' Playboys was etched on a set of drums.

The sun sank lazily and twilight stretched across the courthouse lawn. Shadows lurked here and there. The streetlights provided ample illumination in the warm evening heat. Sweat kissed her skin and she wanted something to drink. Almost on cue, Jody hurried back with a bag of popcorn and a tall plastic cup.

"I could only carry one of each, so we have to share."

"Deal," Peyton replied, reaching for the drink and wondering again why Jody wasn't with the other kids, who were chasing one another around the courthouse in shorts, t-shirts and bare feet. Jody wore jeans and sneakers. Peyton hadn't seen her in anything else.

"Why aren't you playing?" Peyton asked. "The kids are having lots of fun."

Jody dove into the popcorn, head down. "They don't like me and I don't like them."

Why? Peyton wondered. She would have thought that the sheriff's kid would be popular.

The band broke into a tune, and couples headed for the concrete entrance to the courthouse to dance.

"I'm going closer so I can watch." Jody jumped to her feet. "Wanna come?"

"No, thanks."

Jody ran off and Peyton saw her sit on the grass for a good view. By herself. She seemed so lonely. Wyatt danced by with the dark-haired woman in his arms. Jody waved. Even though the sheriff's kid wasn't popular, the sheriff sure was.

She was so engrossed in watching everyone that she didn't notice that Wyatt had stopped dancing until he sat by her with two cups of ice cream.

"Vanilla or peach." He held the cups out to her.

"Peach."

He handed her the peach. A plastic spoon was stuck in the middle and she removed it, then scooped out a bite.

"Mmm. This is delicious," she murmured. "And cold."

"Eat slowly or you'll get brain freeze."

They ate in silence for a minute, then unable to resist, she asked, "Were you dancing with your girlfriend?"

He extended his long legs in front of him. "Marlene? No. Her husband has two left feet and she always tracks me down for dancing. She loves to dance and Wilbur's not jealous of me."

"Oh." She nibbled on the spoon. "Why not?"

He finished off the ice cream and glanced at her. "The whole town knows how I felt about my wife."

"So? She's dead, isn't she?" The words were out before she could drag them back.

His eyes darkened. "Don't stick your nose in my life or my business."

She licked the spoon and decided silence was her best defense. That or dump the remaining ice cream over his head. And she wanted the ice cream.

At Mae's instigation, the band began to play "Jailhouse Rock." All the kids tried to jitterbug. Mae clapped her hands and joined them. Jody sat watching.

Peyton wanted to bring up Jody and her issue with being a girl, but that wasn't her business, either. The whole Carson family seemed to be in denial. What did she know? She'd been the same, but looking at grief from another angle, she had a clearer view of just how destructive it was.

Stuart came up and Wyatt got to his feet. They talked business. Evidently Lamar was back and Wyatt would not have to go in tonight.

As Stuart walked away, Wyatt said, "Jody's about to fall asleep. We better go."

Peyton rose to her feet without a word. Within minutes they were in the car. Jody sat in the front and Mae and Peyton in the back. By the time they reached the house, which was two blocks away, Jody was sound asleep.

Wyatt carried her into the house and to her bedroom.

Mae headed for her room. "I'm so pooped I might not even need Elvis's music to go to sleep. See y'all in the morning."

"'Night, Mae," Peyton said, and walked into Jody's room.

Wyatt laid Jody on her bed and Peyton removed Jody's sneakers. "I can put my child to bed!" Wyatt snapped.

Peyton didn't stop until she had both sneakers and socks off. "Take a chill pill, Sheriff. I'm just helping. I'm not trying to steal her."

As he opened his mouth, she added, "And don't say you don't need my help, because you're getting it." She went to Jody's dresser and brought back her pajamas, the ones with horses on them.

Not another word was said as they wiggled the pajamas onto Jody's limp body. Wyatt pulled the sheet over his daughter.

"'Night, sunshine." He kissed her and then strolled from the room.

Peyton shook her head, grabbed her dollar store T-shirt and

headed for the bathroom, hoping Wyatt wasn't in there. He wasn't. She took a quick bath and returned to the bedroom to do her nightly ritual. Applying lotion to her body and face, she realized she hadn't worn makeup since she'd been here.

At first it had been because of the mosquito bites, but now that the bites were healing, she didn't see any reason to. Glancing closely at herself in the mirror, she liked what she saw—a clear, healthy complexion. Maybe there was something to this wholesome living.

Crawling into bed, she paused. She was thirsty. The hotdog must have been salty. She tiptoed to the door and made her way to the kitchen.

The light was on and she stopped in the doorway. Wyatt sat at the table drinking a beer in the jeans, shirt and boots he'd worn to the party. She didn't say anything, just went to the refrigerator for milk. After pouring a glass, she thought about the chocolate-chip cookies Mae kept in the pantry. She brought them and the milk to the table and sat down.

Wyatt still hadn't said a word.

She dunked a cookie into the milk and took a bite, feeling his eyes on her.

"You have a healthy appetite," he remarked.

She swallowed another bite. "My dad used to say that."

"Is he still living?"

"No. He died five years ago." The milk suddenly seemed to curdle in her stomach.

Wyatt saw the pain that crossed her face. He knew that look well. "I'm sorry," he immediately said.

She shifted into a cross-legged position. "Thank you. You're not the only one who's lost someone they love."

He wanted to tell her it wasn't the same thing, but could see her pain was just as real. "What happened?"

"He died of colon cancer."

He started to apologize for prying. After all, he'd told her his life was none of her business, and hers was certainly none of his.

But she began talking. "I was very close to my father. My mother was always busy with her political aspirations, working on many campaigns. Sometimes she was gone for weeks at a time, but my dad was there to take me to school and pick me up. He helped with my homework and put me to bed by reading stories in his wonderful, soothing voice."

She took a swallow of milk. "When I went to college, I had a room at the sorority house, but I stayed mostly at home. I didn't want him to be alone when my mom was away."

"So you've always lived at home?"

"I had just graduated college and was looking for a condo when he was diagnosed with cancer. I couldn't leave then. At the end, he had around-the-clock nurses, but I was there reading those boring, endless volumes he enjoyed. I never left."

"Sounds as if you loved him a great deal."

"Yes." She ran her thumb down the outside of the glass. "His death was so hard to accept. My mom and I went to Europe afterward to try to heal, but we still had to come back to that house. We had it completely redecorated, but it didn't ease the pain."

"You had time to say goodbye, at least." The words were unexpected and they startled him.

"Many times." She looked at him with darkened, sad eyes.

"I never had a chance to say goodbye to Lori." Again, the words seem to come of their own volition and he was powerless to stop them.

Their gazes held and he understood everything he saw in the blue, liquid depths.

"For what it's worth, it wouldn't have helped."

"What?" For a moment he was lost in her pain.

"Saying goodbye didn't lessen my pain. Nothing did."

He stood and crushed the empty beer can in his hand. Tossing it into the trash, he said, "I'm always going to love her and I'm always going to miss her." He strolled toward the door, needing his space. At the door he stopped. "I'm sorry I snapped at you earlier."

She nodded as if she understood.

PEYTON WASHED her glass and placed it on the drainer. Wyatt and Lori had had a love that was rare, but she wondered, though, how a man like Wyatt could live the rest of his life without falling in love again.

The answer was clear.

By not allowing himself.

And she thought that was the saddest thing of all.

Chapter Fifteen

The next morning the Carsons missed Sunday school and were in a rush to make it to the church service. Peyton didn't have anything else to do, so she decided to go along. It had been a long time since she'd been in a church. She and her father used to go with Grandma Ross when she'd been alive. That had been twelve years ago.

Jody watched as Peyton applied eyeliner. "Why you putting that on?"

"Because—" she paused to think about the question "—it makes me look pretty."

"Yuck."

She let that pass as she reached for the pink strapless sundress with the tiny white band across the top of the bodice she'd planned to wear in Dallas at the party—minus the white, capped-sleeved jacket. She never wore the jacket, but today she would, for modesty's sake.

Jody's eyes were glued to Peyton.

"You have funny underwear."

"So I've been told." She wriggled into the tight-fitting dress.

"Why are you wearing that?"

"I want to wear a dress to church."

"It's too short."

Peyton pulled at the hem, which was way above her knees. "You think so?"

"Yep."

Peyton always thought the shorter the better. For Horseshoe, her thinking might have to change.

"I don't have anything else."

"Wear your slacks like me."

Jody had traded her jeans for black slacks and a white blouse.

"Let's go!" Wyatt called.

"No time," Peyton said, slipping into white heels. She applied a touch of lipstick and ran a brush through her hair. She grabbed her jacket and followed Jody.

Wyatt and Mae glanced at her, but neither said a word, which was just as well. Peyton didn't want to remind them this wasn't 1960.

The church was less than two blocks away. It was a historic white clapboard with gothic windows, just like she'd seen in magazines of old country churches. A steeple with a bell tower reached toward the sky and a cross adorned the top.

Newer rooms had been added to one side. A covered walkway connected them.

As they got out of the car the bell clanged loudly.

"Jimmy Hornsby overdoes that bell," Mae muttered as they went up the wooden steps and through the double doors.

The church was small with pews on both sides. Red carpet ran down the center of the hardwood floor to the pulpit. Mae hurried to the organ on the left, and Peyton followed Wyatt and Jody into a pew. The church was filling up and the parishioners' stares felt like darts in her back. She resisted the urge to pull down her skirt.

Mae began to play and the choir walked in, followed by the pastor. The choir began to sing "Take My Hand, Precious Lord" and the congregation joined in. After several more hymns, Pastor Roland Johnson took to the pulpit. He talked about living every day according to the Word in faith and in love. Peyton had to admit the sermon was moving.

The pastor then reminded everyone about vacation Bible school that was starting on Monday and the need for children to learn the Word early.

Mae cranked up the organ again and harmonious voices filled the chapel. Peyton didn't have a hymnal, so she didn't sing along, but when they sang "The Old Rugged Cross," she couldn't resist. She loved that song and her voice rang out. Suddenly she realized she was the only one singing.

Oh, no! What have I done?

Jody stared up at her, her mouth gaping. Wyatt and the rest of the congregation gazed at her with strange, startled looks.

"I'm sorry," she said automatically, but she didn't know what she was sorry for. Singing without permission maybe?

"Ms. Ross, please don't apologize," the pastor said. "That was lovely."

"Oh. Thank you." No one had ever complimented her voice before, and it made her want to burst into song again.

The congregation made their way outside and paused on the lawn to visit with one another. People didn't seem to be glaring at her so much. Could one song do that?

"Mae, are you ready for Bible school?" Pastor Johnson asked.

"I suppose. I just wished we had more volunteers. Kids from the outlining farms and ranches will be coming."

"Getting help is such a problem." The pastor shook his head. "We still haven't gotten those rooms painted, either, but the Lord will provide all we need."

"I might have the solution to your problem," Wyatt said. "I'll let you know tomorrow."

They walked off, but they didn't go to the car. Instead, they went around the church to a cemetery enclosed with a white picket fence. Wyatt opened the gate, and the family and Peyton walked through. Some of the headstones were weatherworn and old, but the one Wyatt stopped at was relatively new.

Peyton saw the name Lorelei Kay Carson and backed away. This was too personal, too private. Then she saw that it was a double stone and Wyatt's name had already been engraved on it. "Wyatt Presley" didn't even throw her; she'd almost expected it.

All the stone needed was the day of his death.

There was something so wrong about that, but she couldn't explain it. She did know a man his age shouldn't be waiting to etch the day of his death on a headstone. She turned and made her way to the car.

Glancing back, she saw Mae had gone over to another grave—probably Johnny's and her husband's. She wondered if they did this every Sunday. It couldn't be healthy for any of them, especially Jody.

Peyton tried to put the image out of her mind, but it stayed with her. The Carsons were stuck in the past, unable to move forward.

In the afternoon Wyatt and Jody went fishing. Peyton played poker with Mae and her friends, Gladys, Bernice and Freda.

At first the atmosphere was tense, but then Mae said, "She's got money and we're gonna take it, girls. So ante up." Mae shuffled the cards. "And when she loses, she has to model her underwear."

"Mae!" Peyton was shocked.

"What kind of underwear?" Gladys wanted to know.

"You wouldn't believe." Mae dealt the cards. "And if one of us loses, I guess we'll have to model our baggy drawers."

"Fair's fair," Peyton said.

In the end she lost amidst a lot of laughter. She showed her thong, but not the one she was wearing.

"Oh, my God, it's like a slingshot." Bernice stared at the scrap of lace and spandex.

"Now if I had worn underwear like that, ol' Vern might've stayed around a little longer," Freda commented.

"Or have a permanent wedgie," Mae told her.

More discussion followed and Peyton laughed until her sides hurt.

Mae did, too.

Peyton wiped away tears of joy; she didn't feel like an outsider anymore.

ON MONDAY she received new duties. She would be helping out at the church and painting the Sunday-school rooms.

"I don't have a clue how to paint," she told Wyatt.

"You'll learn," was his response.

And she did. But first she helped out with the classes. Angie Wiznowski was a single mom and had a daughter, Erin, the same age as Jody. She had the class for seven- and eight-year olds. Marlene, Wyatt's dancing partner, had a daughter, Bethann, who was also Jody's age. Marlene was in charge of the five- and six-year-olds. Mae and Gladys handled the kids older than ten and Judy, the nurse, taught the three- and four-year-olds.

The moment she saw Judy, Peyton knew what she had to do. After class she went to Judy's room.

"Oh, Peyton," Judy said as she closed Bibles. "Do you need something?"

"Yes. I need to apologize. I'm sorry I was so rude to you."

Judy stored the Bibles away. "After your ordeal, I think you're entitled to be a little rude."

"That's very generous and understanding. Thank you."

Judy smiled. "I hope you enjoy Bible school and your stay in Horseshoe."

Peyton returned her smile. "I'm trying."

"And don't be too hard on poor Wyatt."

Peyton scrunched up her face. "I'll think about that one."

Judy's laugh followed her as she tackled the painting project.

Painting was relatively easy, especially with the roller she'd been given. In the mornings she helped with the classes and in the afternoons she painted. It was working out well. She found she loved working with the kids, and they seemed to like her. It was easy since she was often like a kid herself. The mothers were talking to her, too, and she wasn't treated like an outsider. Or a criminal.

On Thursday Angie got a call that her grandmother had fallen, and she rushed off to take her to the hospital in Temple. She left Peyton in charge of the class. The Bible lesson and reading were over, they sang a few hymns, and then Peyton thought it was time for a change of pace.

"Okay." She clasped her hands. "Ready to have some fun?"

"Yeah!" they shouted.

"Move all the chairs and desks back."

The kids hurried to do her bidding, pushing everything against the wall.

"Anyone know 'Jeremiah Was a Bullfrog'?"

They shook their heads, but they were smiling, even Jody.

"Okay. Sing after me." And Peyton began to sing the lively rock song."

The kids yelled, instead of sang, but that was fine.

She clapped her hands, kept singing the song, and the kids joined in. They were getting into it and she called, "Conga line" pulling Jody behind her and the other kids followed suit. "Everybody sing. Loud! 'Jeremiah…'"

They marched around the room, singing, laughing and having fun. Pastor Roland stood in the doorway with a Texas-size scowl on his face. Peyton saw him and came to a complete stop. The kids bumped into her.

"Ms. Ross, may I see you in the hall, please?" His tone was so sharp it could have cut through a T-bone steak, including the bone.

"Read your Bible verses," he said to the children.

Peyton followed him into the hall. He closed the door and turned to her. "Where is Angie?"

"She had an emergency and had to leave."

"Your actions are highly inappropriate, Ms. Ross. That song is unsuitable for tender ears."

"It was just fun."

"I do not approve of it. The class is just about over, and hopefully Angie will be back tomorrow. Wait with the children until their parents arrive. And no more of that kind of singing."

He walked away with quick steps, his haughty nose stuck in the air. *Good grief, what a...* She didn't finish the thought. She was in church and would exercise good manners.

WYATT KNEW something was wrong when he saw Roland hurrying toward his office.

What's she done now?

He got to his feet as the pastor entered his office.

"Oh, Wyatt, good, you're here," Roland said as he spotted Wyatt. "We have a problem."

How many times had he heard that line concerning Peyton? "What happened?"

"Ms. Ross is not working out."

"You have to give her time, Pastor."

Roland leaned over and whispered, "She's singing inappropriate songs to the children."

Wyatt frowned. "Like what?"

"'Jeremiah Was a Bullfrog.'"

"Excuse me?"

"You know the song. Drinking some wine, real good wine, or something like that. The kids are not there to learn such things. I can't have it. You'll have to find her something else to do."

"Did you ask her to stop?"

"Yes."

"And…?"

"I told her she had to stop and she didn't say anything."

"So the problem is solved."

"Wyatt, it would be best if you found her something else to do."

"Now, Roland, she's very good with the kids. The parents have even commented on it, and frankly, I'm out of options."

"I'm sorry, Wyatt."

He clenched his jaw for a second. "Roland, being a minister and all, you do believe in second chances, don't you?"

"Of course."

"Well, then, that's all Ms. Ross needs."

"Wyatt—"

"She's doing a good job painting the rooms, right?"

"Yes."

"I'll have a talk with her to make sure there are no more misunderstandings."

Roland pointed a finger at him. "You do that. One more chance. That's it."

Wyatt plopped into his chair with a sigh and a curse.

THAT NIGHT Wyatt didn't need an opportunity to bring up the song. Jody was prancing around the house happily singing, *"Jeremiah was a bullfrog."*

"New song?" Wyatt lifted an eyebrow at Peyton when Jody dashed into the living room to watch *Wheel of Fortune*.

She whirled from the sink. "The good pastor spoke to you?"

"Just tone it down. No more singing about wine."

"Does he object to frogs?"

"I don't think so."

She smiled and he felt her warmth in places he didn't want to. "Need help with the dishes?"

"No." She tilted her head. "I'm getting very good at this."

"Especially when there are no pots and pans to wash."

Her mouth fell open and he walked outside and sat on the steps. She quickly followed, sitting by his side, her delicate scent reaching his nostrils, stirring his senses.

"You know?"

"I'd be a very poor detective if I didn't."

She wrapped her arms around her legs. "How long have you known?"

"Years. And when my mom did cook, she was terrible at it. I guess I was eight or so before I knew you didn't cut gravy with a fork."

She laughed, a soft, seductive sound that heightened his awareness of everything around him. He rushed into speech like a callow youth. "When she came up with the brilliant idea of getting food from the diner, my dad said not to look a gift horse in the mouth. It made her happy that we were happy, so not one word was ever said."

"Have you ever thought of telling her that you know and you don't mind?"

"Lori said it was crazy, but a good kind of crazy. That's the way I look at it."

Crickets serenaded and the warm night air wrapped around them. He didn't say anything else. It was just comfortable with her by his side. And *comfortable* wasn't a word he associated with Peyton.

A siren. Gorgeous. Maddening. *Comfortable* just didn't work. Except tonight it did.

PEYTON HATED the color that had been chosen for the classrooms. It reminded her of dirty dishwater, and she was beginning to know that color very well. Wyatt had said it had been donated to the church. She knew why. No one wanted a room that color.

Kids needed something bright and cheerful and Peyton tried to think of a way to give the rooms a little *oomph.* A mural was the first thing that came to mind.

When she was in high school, she'd taken art classes and the class project was a mural in the library. It had been a lot of fun, and the teacher had said that Peyton had a real artistic flair.

It had been so long ago. Could she paint a mural by herself? She went to the general store and found they could order oil paints and brushes. But she knew she couldn't do anything unless she cleared it with the good pastor.

He hesitated when she broached the subject. She got the feeling he thought she might paint something risqué on the wall.

"I'm thinking a serene landscape," she hastened to reassure him.

"What will this cost?"

"Nothing. It will be my gift to the church."

That did the trick. "Just make sure it's something pleasant."

She couldn't believe she was so excited, but she wasn't sure if she remembered much from those art classes. Maybe she should have mentioned that to the pastor.

Over the next few days she worked tirelessly on the project. The scene she chose was of the country church itself sitting among the oaks. She realized that might be out of her realm of talent, but she was going to try.

The first attempt was a disaster. Pastor Johnson eyed what looked like the work of a drunk gone wild.

"Ms. Ross," he said in that sharp, devil-beware tone.

"Okay. I know it's bad, but I can fix it."

"Ms. Ross." His tone softened a bit. "I don't believe painting a mural is your forte. But I'd very much like for you to think about singing a solo in church."

"Oh." That surprised and delighted her at the same time.

"A hymn," he added for clarity.

"Sure. I'd love to, but please let me finish the mural. I'll start over."

"Ms. Ross…"

"At my own expense and in my own time."

He agreed halfheartedly. "Okay, but don't make me regret it."

After class, she couldn't wait to get to the project. She painted over her first attempt with a soft rust color. The next day she drew trees and the country church on the wall. She had to draw it at least four times before she was satisfied she had everything in the right place and the right size.

The next day she picked up the paint she'd ordered from the general store and started on the sky. The kids from the farms and ranches who had to wait for their parents to pick them up started drifting in to watch, and then they wanted to help. Erin and Bethann begged their mothers to let them stay. Of course Jody was like her shadow, and before long they had an after-class project going.

They wanted to sing "Jeremiah" while they painted, so Peyton figured out a way to do that. As she painted the cerulean-blue sky, she sang the song and the kids joined her.

When they came to the wine part, she pointed to nine-year-old Matt.

"Kool-Aid," he sang.

"Soda pop," Bethann shouted.

"Root beer," Erin said.

"Milk," Jody sang, laughing, and Peyton thought how wonderful it sounded.

"Oh, yeah. Some really, really good milk," she sang.

They all dissolved into laughter.

After a moment Matt asked, "Ms. Ross, can we put Jeremiah in the mural?"

"I don't see why not, except I don't know if I can draw a frog. Can anyone draw a frog?"

"I can," Jody answered.

"I'll help," Matt offered.

Jody frowned. "I don't—"

"Jody would love your help." Peyton intervened quickly. "Let's see, where should we put him?"

Jody knelt on the floor. "How about here in the corner in the grass?"

"Perfect." Peyton clapped her hands.

Matt knelt by Jody and they went to work drawing a frog on paper first.

Peyton sighed and felt a happiness she'd never felt before. She felt wanted, needed and appreciated. She swung around and saw Wyatt standing in the doorway, watching the scene. That happiness intensified tenfold.

Then it hit her.

She'd fallen in love with the sheriff of Horseshoe, Texas.

A man who was in love with his dead wife.

Chapter Sixteen

Life had settled down in Horseshoe, Wyatt thought as he marked another day off the calendar. Peyton had found her groove and it made his life a whole lot easier. She loved kids and they loved her. Finally he wasn't getting any more complaints. Her time in Horseshoe would soon be over.

He couldn't figure out why that made him sad. He'd been marking off hours as if they were his own personal sentence, so what was his problem?

Leaning back in his chair, he had to admit that Peyton had burrowed her way into his heart. She never gave up and he admired that. She'd morphed from a rich, spoiled young woman into someone he liked and…

The woman was crazy, absolutely crazy.

Each day he could feel her craziness affecting him—more and more.

WYATT FOUND he enjoyed going home these days. There wasn't so much sadness in the house. Peyton didn't give them time for that.

Peyton went shopping for groceries with his mom, and before he knew it, his mother was cooking again—stuff out of jars and boxes, maybe, but Peyton and his mom were learning together. Spaghetti sauce out of a jar, garlic bread out of the freezer section, salad out of a bag, but once it was put together they had a home-cooked meal.

Jody told him the big secret. "You have to follow directions." And it usually required a lot of laughter.

When he came home, it wasn't to Elvis's music. It was to laughter.

Getting out of his car, he smiled at the sight in front of him. Peyton, Jody and his mom were giving Dolittle a bath in a large kiddie pool. Where the pool had come from he had no idea, but he knew Peyton had something to do with it.

All three of them were wearing shorts and T-shirts. His mom's reached her knees. They were singing "Hound Dog."

Dolittle had had enough. He bolted for freedom, shaking water off as he loped away. They didn't chase him. Instead, they lounged in the pool of water that was only about twelve inches deep.

"Hey, Daddy." Jody spotted him. "We're chilling."

"I see."

"Supper will be ready in thirty minutes, son," his mom said. "Take a load off."

"I'll just…" Wyatt didn't know what to say. He was in shock that his mom was in the water.

"Join us, Daddy," Jody called, splashing her feet.

"I have things to do."

"Don't be so stuffy, son," Mae said.

"He needs a little incentive," Peyton said, and before he knew her intention, she picked up the hose and sprayed him.

He jumped back, staring at the water on the front of his clothes. "Hey!"

She sprayed him again.

Jody laughed, as did his mom.

He made a dive for the hose, but Peyton leaped away and ran with it, turning to spray him as he tried to catch her. Finally he grabbed the hose and reeled her in like a fish. But he never saw a fish like her. Blue eyes sparkled with mischief and her wet T-shirt boldly outlined the fullness of her breasts. Clearly she wasn't wearing a bra. Desire ignited deep in his gut.

"Peyton got you good, Daddy," Jody declared as she climbed out of the pool.

Yeah, Peyton got him good in more ways than he wanted to admit.

WYATT WAS BEGINNING to enjoy Peyton's craziness. As he made his way home, he wondered what to expect. His family and Peyton weren't in the yard, so he hurried through the back door and came to a complete stop. Peyton wasn't in the kitchen as usual, helping his mom. He felt a moment of loneliness, which was absurd.

Jody sat at the table, drawing something on paper. His mom was putting ice in glasses.

"Hi, son," his mom said. "Supper will be ready—" she looked at her watch "—in fifteen minutes. Peyton and I are trying a roast in the crockpot and we're following directions to the letter." Mae shook her head. "I don't know what she'll have me doing next."

"Where is she?"

"She's still at the church, working on that mural," Mae replied. "Had some detail she wanted to finish."

"It'll be dark soon. I'll go get her."

"I'd go, too, Daddy, but I'm drawing Jeremiah. I can't get his feet the way I want. We're going to paint him on the mural on Monday, so I have to get it right."

Wyatt kissed the top of her head. "Okay, sunshine."

"Don't jiggle me, Daddy."

"Oh, pardon me." Wyatt left with a smile on his face.

It took less than five minutes to reach the church. Peyton was on the ladder, engrossed in her work. The mural was coming along nicely, although it had a primitive feel to it. The old country church sat among big oak trees under a blue sky. Green grasses dotted the foreground. It wasn't finished yet, but it was clear what it was going to be.

"Hey, Van Gogh, you ready for supper?"

"Very funny." She didn't pause to look at him. "I just want to finish putting this lighter green on the leaves so it will be dry tomorrow. There. Done." One foot reached for a rung.

This is where she trips and falls into my arms, he thought. At least, that was the way it happened in the movies. But Peyton deftly came down the ladder without missing a rung.

And he was disappointed.

"I'll clean the brushes, close the paints and then we can be on our way."

"That will take time."

She cocked an eyebrow and the gesture shot through him with the power of a .38 Special. "Not if you help."

"Oh, no. This isn't my project."

She reached for his hand and pulled him into the small back room where she had all the painting paraphernalia stored. "I wash dishes. You can wash brushes."

"It's not the same thing."

Smiling, she dragged one finger down his nose—a finger smeared with paint. He felt its wetness and its pungent scent—but most of all he felt the punch of her smile. "Why you…"

She darted into the next room and he chased her around chairs and desks and finally had to leap over a chair before he snagged her. Their laughter bounced off the walls…and then suddenly there was quiet. He gazed into her blue eyes and was lost in feelings he'd forgotten.

Or kept buried.

Of their own volition his hands cupped her face and his lips lowered to hers, tasting her softness, her eagerness. But he wanted more. He needed more. With a groan, he captured her lips completely and everything faded away except the touch and feel of her.

Of Peyton.

The kiss went on and on, and he threaded his fingers through her hair as it tumbled around her shoulders. Her hands touched his neck and a shiver shot through him—a shiver of longing and lust.

Lust—that was all it was. Lori's face drifted across his mind and he tore his mouth away.

"I'm sorry. That shouldn't have happened." He wiped his mouth, but he couldn't wipe away the feel of her.

"Wyatt—"

"We need to go."

As if reading his mind, she said, "Lori's dead, Wyatt. You're alive."

"Don't say her name."

She swung toward the back room and they cleaned the brushes in silence. Then they scrubbed the paint from their faces.

Not one word was said on the drive to the house. He'd hurt her and that was the last thing he'd wanted. He was bombarded with so many feelings and he couldn't voice any of them—only the one that mattered to him. *He loved his wife; he would always love Lori.*

Luckily when they reached the house, Jody monopolized the conversation and Peyton was back to her bubbly self.

But Wyatt couldn't leave it at that.

His mom was engrossed in an Elvis movie. Peyton and Jody were getting ready for bed. He knocked at the door and went in.

He kissed his daughter. "'Night, sunshine."

"'Night, Daddy," Jody mimicked, wiggling in the bed. "I drew a good Jeremiah. Yes, I did. Yeah. Oh, yeah."

Jody never used to sing, but now she was bursting at the seams with songs.

All because of Peyton.

He drew a heavy breath and his eyes collided with Peyton's. "May I speak to you, please?"

"Why?" Alarmed, Jody sat up. "She didn't do anything wrong."

Now she had Jody as her champion. "It's business, sunshine. Go to sleep."

"Okay," she replied, but there was hesitation in her voice as if she didn't quite believe him.

He walked out of the room to the backyard. He wanted privacy for what he had to say.

The door opened and she slipped out, sitting on the step. "Make this short. I prefer the air-conditioning."

He paced in front of her. "I'm sorry for what happened."

"Now there's a shocker."

"I'm trying to discuss this with you."

Peyton jammed her T-shirt over her knees. "Well, maybe I don't want to discuss it with you."

"I'm the sheriff and you're in my care and—"

"Oh, please. Don't even go there or I might be forced to smack you."

"I love my wife."

"I think you've mentioned that a time or two. This would be a really interesting conversation if the woman was alive." The words were cruel, but Peyton couldn't stop herself. "She's dead, Wyatt, and you're a living, breathing man with needs. And I can tell you those needs are screaming for expression."

"Don't—"

She jumped to her feet. "Don't tell me one more time not to say her name."

The evening breeze caressed the heat in her cheeks and made her aware of how angry she was. And she wasn't taking back a single word. In fact, she was in a mood to add more.

"I thought I was in denial about my father's death, but you actually make me look sane. You take your eight-year-old daughter to visit her mother's grave every Sunday. How depressing is that for a child? For heaven's sake, do you think your wife would want you to live like this? You're not living, you're just existing, marking time until someone can etch the date of your death on a stone."

"Shut up!"

She whirled for the door and he grabbed her, jerking her into his arms. Tension and anger throbbed through him, but she didn't feel his anger as his lips captured hers. They were gentle, soft and seductive. The passionate touch made her melt, and she was glad he was holding her or she would have melted to the ground in a puddle. The emotions were that strong, that hot.

She could actually feel the heat simmering between them, heat he'd kept buried deep inside him. But she felt it now and it scorched both of them.

Her response was immediate. Her hands tangled in his hair as he pulled her closer, their tongues mingling in a hot, bothered and ready dance.

His hands slid beneath her T-shirt and caressed her back, her breasts. She moaned as his thumb tantalized one nipple with provocative strokes.

She felt every muscle of his hard body and the world was slowly, wonderfully spinning away to where only lovers were welcome.

Lovers!

The word gave Peyton pause. She wanted his love. She wanted it all. She did not want to be just a stand-in for Lori. Or just for some need he had to fill.

With more strength than she thought she had, she drew back, licked her lips and took a moment to breathe. To think. His musky, manly scent coated every awakened nerve and she didn't want to move away, to lose that feeling, that special connection. But she did.

The past was like a veil between them, thin and fragile. And impenetrable. A door slammed and cars hummed on the highway. All she heard, though, was his ragged breathing. Or was that her own?

She drew a hard breath and said what she had to. "That's living and feeling. Think about it." Then she bolted for the door.

WYATT SANK onto the step and dragged in each precious breath. He tried to bring up Lori's face and he couldn't. That scared him. His peaceful world, his shrine to Lori, was slipping away and he was powerless to stop it. He wasn't sure he wanted to. That frightened him even more.

You're just existing, marking time.

Peyton was right. That was what he was doing and it wasn't healthy for him. Or for Jody.

So what did he do about it?

Right now, he wasn't sure about anything, except all the raw emotions Peyton had awakened in him. Her taste was still on his tongue and his nostrils were filled with her scent.

He tugged his hands through his hair, cursing that he had no control where she was concerned. And he should have control.

Peyton Ross wasn't the woman for him.

Chapter Seventeen

The townspeople gathered on the courthouse lawn for their monthly Saturday party and to celebrate the Fourth of July. Peyton didn't sit on a bench and watch. She worked her butt off helping Angie and Marlene make popcorn and serve drinks.

"You're so good at this," Angie said, watching Peyton scoop popcorn into a brown bag.

Peyton winked. "I can wash dishes, too. Not that I'm volunteering or anything."

Angie laughed, handing Mrs. Hornsby a drink. "Peyton, you've brought excitement to this sleepy town."

She didn't know about that. All she knew was that she was happy, something she hadn't been in a while.

Judge Fitzwater, dressed in plaid shorts and a polo shirt, walked up and ordered a drink. "Ms. Ross, you're doing a very fine job in Horseshoe."

"Thank you."

The D.A. ambled over. "Save a dance for me, Peyton."

"You got it."

Marlene frowned. "Now, Hardy Beckham, you never tell *me* that."

Hardy bowed from the waist. "My sincere apologies."

"Yeah, right." Marlene laughed, and then whispered to Peyton, "Men are such idiots."

Lamar, who was on duty, nervously stepped up. "Ms. Ross, I'm so sorry about the jailbreak and what you had to go through."

"Thank you. I'm just happy you're okay."

"Still—"

"Lamar, stop worrying about it. I'm fine. You're fine, and Zeke is where he should be."

She hated that he blamed himself, but he seemed in a better mood as he walked away.

Later, she and the kids, who all seemed to be attached to her, sat on the lawn and ate hot dogs and watermelon.

No one ignored her. When folks walked by, they'd shout, "Hey, Peyton, how's the mural coming?" Or, "Peyton, when you gonna help out at my place?" She laughed and joked with them as if she'd lived here all her life.

She had once thought that the people here were poor, but now she knew they were rich beyond measure with family, friends and love. And Peyton felt a part of this very rich community.

The band broke into "Louisiana Saturday Night" and everyone gathered to dance. But not before Peyton and the kids did their rendition of "Jeremiah Was a Bullfrog." Everyone was in stitches. Jody didn't just sit and watch, either. She participated, and then Erin, Bethann and Jody danced together, holding hands. Jody was making friends and it was wonderful to see. They hadn't talked about her resistance to being called a girl, and Peyton was hoping it would simply fade away.

After a while Peyton was out of breath from dancing with Virgil, Ramrod, Hardy and several other men. But the one man she wanted to dance with wasn't there.

She and Wyatt had talked little since they'd shared the passionate kiss in the moonlight. She could tell he wanted to apologize and she was grateful he didn't. Because that might cause her to really smack him.

Soon her time here would be up and she would go back to her life in Austin. Giselle hadn't called since that one time, and neither had Mindy or Bree. They would now be a part of her past. There would also be no more parties, heavy drinking or throwing hissy fits when she didn't get her way.

She had truly grown up in this small country town. And fallen in love. She would return to Austin with a broken heart because Wyatt Carson was not ready to move forward. She feared he never would be.

Virgil stepped on her toes and Peyton said, "Ouch."

"Sorry about that, sugar."

"It's okay. I think I'm about danced out."

"I'll take over." Wyatt moved from the shadows, and her heart rate went into overdrive.

"Hey, Sheriff," Virgil said, placing her hand in Wyatt's. "Ms. Peyton is ready for someone to sweep her off her feet. Lord knows I've bruised them enough."

She moved into Wyatt's arms and they sailed across the concrete. He wore jeans, white shirt, boots and his Stetson. The manly scent she associated with him trapped her in her own private paradise.

They didn't speak. They didn't need to. For once they just enjoyed the feeling of being together.

The waltz ended and a slower number began. Now Peyton rested her head on his chest and they swayed, barely moving.

"You smell great," he said softly.

"Are you flirting with me?" She looked up into his face.

"Is that possible?" He smiled and it was one of the most beautiful sights she'd ever seen. He didn't smile enough. It softened the strong angles of his face and made him look vulnerable. Made him all male and that much more attractive.

"Oh, yeah, Sheriff, it's possible. Just remember I'm not easy."

"Never crossed my mind."

She sighed with pure happiness as the song came to an end. As did the evening.

But not before everyone sang "God Bless the U.S.A."

On the drive back to the house, Jody clamored for her daddy's attention and Peyton was just happy to watch them. He was different tonight. He seemed happy.

Was there hope?

At home Mae went to her room and Peyton followed Jody to theirs. She glanced back and caught Wyatt's eyes—a silent goodnight of attraction and need. She kept searching for the love.

She didn't find it and quietly closed the door.

Jody had the bathroom first and then Peyton. When she entered the bedroom, Jody was peering into Peyton's makeup bag in her suitcase.

Peyton noticed her phone and iPod. She hadn't used either in days. She'd once thought she couldn't live without a bud in her ear or text-messaging like crazy. Suddenly life was so different. And it wasn't bad, not at all.

"I didn't touch anything," Jody said quickly. Dolittle barked as if to reassure her that Jody hadn't.

Peyton sat on the floor by her bag. "You can touch anything you want."

"Can I touch that?" She pointed to a tube of lipstick.

"Sure." Peyton pulled off the cap. "It's called Very Berry Good. Isn't that cool? Here." She quickly applied the color to Jody's lips before she could pull away. When Jody didn't protest, Peyton fluffed out her short blond hair. Then she surveyed her handiwork.

"Mmm. Take a peek in the mirror."

Jody stood and stared, wide-eyed, at herself.

"What do you think?"

"I look like…a girl."

"Yes."

Suddenly in tears, Jody scrubbed at her lips and slicked down her hair. "I'm not a girl!" she cried, and ran to her bed. She curled up in a fetal position.

Peyton rose to her feet, not sure what to do, but knowing she had to do something. This little girl was hurting.

Stepping onto her bed, Peyton hoisted herself onto Jody's. She rested her back against the wall. Dolittle leaped up beside her, turning several times before he settled by Jody.

"Jody, you are a girl, a very pretty girl. You favor your mother."

"I'm not a girl. I can't be a girl."

Peyton was lost. All she could do was feel her way. First she gathered Jody into her arms and held her. The thin body trembled and Peyton prayed for the right words.

"It's just you and I in this room. Well, Do's here, but he's not talking." She stroked Jody's hair. "Tell me why you can't be a girl."

"I can't." Jody rubbed her face against Peyton. "I can't tell anyone."

"We're friends, aren't we?"

Jody nodded. "I don't not like you anymore." Realizing that sounded weird, she added, "You know what I mean."

"Yes, I do." She kissed Jody's cheek. "Friends trust each other and tell each other everything, even if it hurts."

"Do they?"

"They sure do."

Peyton waited, but Jody remained quiet.

"Why can't you be a girl?" she asked, holding her breath.

"Because…because they'll take me away."

Peyton was confused. "Who are they?"

"I don't…"

Peyton cupped Jody's face and made her look at her. "Who are they?"

"One time—" she hiccupped "—Grandma's sister, Aunt Nell, her daughter and another woman, I don't remember her name, came to visit."

"And?"

"I heard them talking. They were talking about Daddy and how much he loved my mama. They said it was a shame Jody wasn't a boy 'cause then my daddy wouldn't have a problem raising me. And…and it might be best if someone took Jody and raised her. That way Daddy wouldn't be reminded of Mama. So you see—" Jody burrowed into her "—I can't be a girl. They'll take me."

Peyton was appalled. "Jody, listen to me. You know your daddy loves you. No one would take you away from him."

Jody raised her head and Peyton saw the doubt and insecurity of an eight-year-old child.

"Oh, you're afraid your daddy will send you away."

Jody nodded. "I remind him of Mama and—"

"No, no, no." Peyton gripped Jody tightly. "The fact that you look like your mama is one of the things your daddy loves about you. He treasures that. No one will ever, ever take you away from him. He would die first. I've only been here a short while, but I know that without a shadow of a doubt."

Jody raised her head. "You do?"

"Oh, yes." Peyton wiped a tear from Jody's cheek. "I'm sorry you had to overhear that, but it was just women talking about something they know nothing about. Sometimes women do that."

"Like talking to hear their brains rattle."

"Mmm." Peyton lifted an eyebrow. "A Virgil and Ramrod saying?"

"Yep."

Peyton looked into eyes, so like Wyatt's, and felt warmth stirring inside her. "So, babycakes, are you a girl?"

Jody face puckered. "Babycakes? Yuck. I'm not a baby."

"Sweet cheeks?"

"Double yuck."

Peyton narrowed her eyes in thought. "So what would be a really good nickname?"

"Jody girl." A smile curved Jody's mouth and Peyton considered it a big breakthrough.

"Well, Jody girl—" Peyton kissed her cheek again "—time for bed."

Jody scrambled beneath the sheet and Peyton slid down to her bed. Then she crossed the room and flipped off the light.

"This is our secret, right, Peyton?"

"Right."

"On Monday Matt and I are drawing Jeremiah on the mural. Oh, yeah. 'Jeremiah was…'" Jody's voice drifted away into little girl's dreams.

Peyton tossed and turned, unable to sleep, and she knew why. Even though it was told in secret, she had to tell Wyatt what Jody had revealed. He had to know what his daughter had been going through. She eased from the bed and quietly slipped out of the room.

She paused at Wyatt's closed door. Maybe it could wait until morning. No, it couldn't. Biting her lip, she opened the door and stepped inside. The room was in total darkness. It took a moment to get her bearings and then she saw Wyatt lying on his side, the sheet pulled to his waist. He was sound asleep.

Drawing a quick breath, she tiptoed to the bed and touched

his shoulder. In an instant she was flat on her back in the bed beside him, being held down with a strong arm.

"What the hell are you doing?" he snapped.

"Trying to breathe."

He removed his arm from her chest. "What are you doing here?"

She sat up and shoved her fingers through her hair. "I wanted to talk to you. I wasn't planning on getting pinned to the bed."

Rising to a sitting position, he scooted up against the headboard. "Sorry. It's a reflex."

She turned to face him, sitting back on her heels. His chest was bare, as it had been that day she'd seen him in the bathroom. Her fingers itched to reach out and touch those rippling muscles, to feel their strength, their...

Okay, this wasn't the reason she was here. *Get a grip, Peyton. You've been around men before. But not one who touched all your sensory buttons by just the look in his eyes.*

"Can't this wait until morning?"

What? Oh, she quickly reined in her wandering thoughts. "It's about Jody."

He was instantly alert. "Is she sick? What's wrong?" He made to get out of the bed and she caught his arm, and then wished she hadn't. His naked skin felt so smooth....

"She's fine." She bulldozed into speech before she made a fool of herself. "I hope you won't be upset, but I talked to her about her insistence that she's not a girl."

"And?" His voice didn't sound angry, just curious.

Relaxing, she told him what Jody had told her.

"Those interfering old biddies. They had no right. Why didn't Jody tell me?" He swung his feet to the floor. "I have to talk to my daughter."

"Wait." Peyton grabbed him and pulled him back onto the

bed. "I promised Jody that it's our secret. She trusts me and I don't want her to know I told you."

"Like hell. Jody has to hear from me that I love her and nothing or no one will ever take her away from me."

"We talked and she knows that. Give her time and I believe you'll see a change."

"She's not your daughter. She's mine." She felt his anger like a slap in the face as he leaped from the bed and reached for his jeans, which lay over a chair.

"If you break the trust she has in me, you'll hurt her. And you'll hurt me."

He stared at his jeans for a moment and then threw them into the chair, knocking it over with a resounding thud. "I don't understand why she wouldn't tell me."

"Because she's eight years old and afraid."

He sank onto the bed. "Lori and I had our lives all planned, except we never planned on Lori not being here."

It was the first time he'd ever volunteered anything about his wife to her. She scooted to sit beside him.

"I know the feeling. I never thought my dad wouldn't be here to guide me with his wonderful advice. He won't walk me down the aisle, either, something we both dreamed about."

"Does it get any easier?"

"For me, at last, it has." She smoothed the T-shirt over her thighs. "Since I've been here in Horseshoe, facing reality, I haven't felt that crippling pain. I've been really *facing* my life and that's helped. I'm embarrassed to say my dad would have been disappointed in me for acting like I was, but the truth is he was the king of pampering and I milked that for all it was worth."

"You're very honest."

"Yeah, when you have to wash dishes and clean toilets it kind of brings everything else into perspective."

A silence fell between them. Not uncomfortable, yet there as if neither knew what to say next. Or were afraid to admit what they were thinking. Finally Peyton dove right in. To her, it was all or nothing.

"How do you think Lori would feel about the way you're living your life?" She braced herself for his anger, but it didn't come.

"We promised to love each other forever and I intend to keep that promise."

Her heart rocked with pain. But she refused to give up. "So you think she'd be happy that you're not living, just existing?"

He stood, his pajama bottoms low on his hips. She could see that from the moonlight sneaking through the blinds. "You don't understand the relationship we had."

"No. Not if it's destroying you now." She gulped at her own audacity. "If Lori was the type of woman you say she was, then I know she would want you to be happy. She'd certainly want her child to be happy."

He didn't say anything, just stared at the crisscross patterns of the muted moonlight. Then his voice came from somewhere deep within him. "So many times I wished it had been me, instead of her, and then Jody would have had her mother."

Peyton crawled off the bed and walked to his side, suddenly seeing a lot of things she hadn't before. "Stop punishing yourself for being alive."

"Peyton—"

"That's what you're doing." She placed a hand on his bare arm. "I feel a living, breathing man who has punished himself too long."

He stiffened. "Please go back to your room."

"Why?"

He looked at her then and she felt the heat and the restraint he was putting on himself. "You know I want you."

"I want you, too."

"Peyton." He sighed heavily.

"I'm not asking anything of you." She ran her hand up his arm to his shoulder. "But to just let yourself feel again."

His arm snaked out and he pulled her to him, and the moment her skin touched his, they forgot everything else.

With moans and sighs they fell backward on to the bed. Her T-shirt and his pajama bottoms landed on the floor, and then there was nothing between them but that veil of the past they'd managed to penetrate.

Wyatt was a starving man and he ate and drank his fill of the most sensual woman he'd ever touched. Her skin was softer, her sighs deeper and her kisses so intoxicating that he wasn't sure he was sober.

"Protection," he managed in a moment of lucidity.

"Sorority girls are always protected." A bubbly laugh escaped her throat and the world as he knew it spun away.

She wanted him to feel. And he did. Every scintillating inch of her. When her cries of fulfillment reached his ears, he trembled from the pleasure and followed her into the release that his body had been craving.

And not once did he think of Lori.

Only Peyton.

Chapter Eighteen

Much, much later, Peyton luxuriated in the warm, giddy afterglow. Without shame. Their lovemaking had exceeded everything she'd ever thought possible. When it was so right, it was so powerful.

But what happened next?

Her back curled into Wyatt's chest and his arm rested across her waist. His warm breath fanned her hair. At this moment, everything was idyllic, perfect. What dreams were made of.

The morning light would bring reality, though. For Wyatt it would bring guilt, Peyton was sure. He'd given in to his baser instincts and he was going to hate himself for betraying Lori's love. Peyton knew him that well. It didn't take someone with a psychology degree to figure that one out.

Closing her eyes, she memorized the sensation of his naked skin against hers. Regrets she would leave to Wyatt. For her, last night had been exactly what she wanted. And she wouldn't apologize for that.

Gently, she removed his arm and slid from the bed. She didn't want Jody to wake up and find her gone. That was the trouble with growing up—it made a person responsible. Weeks ago she wouldn't have cared.

She turned her gaze to him and soaked up that relaxed, sated look on his handsome face. A look their lovemaking had put there. But the word *love* had never been mentioned. She wanted to lean over and kiss him to feel the stubble that shadowed his face, but he'd awaken. She wasn't ready to see the guilt in his eyes. For now she'd take the look on his face to signify that last night had meant something to him.

That was all she needed for now.

She found her T-shirt and pulled it over her head. It took a while to find her panties, though. Finally she saw the hot pink sticking out from the sheet. After easing them free, she moved toward the door. She stopped and blew him a kiss, reluctant to tear her eyes away from his beautiful, sleeping form. She wondered if she'd ever see him like that again.

WYATT AWOKE with a smile. He stretched, ready to tackle the day with an energy he hadn't felt in ages. Then he caught sight of his pajama bottoms lying halfway across the room on the hardwood floor.

Oh, no! What had he done? He pushed himself to a sitting position. Last night came back in vivid Technicolor detail. Peyton—her beautiful face, her sensuous smile, her deep sighs, her breathless moans, her seductive touch that had awakened parts of him he'd sworn were dead forever.

They belonged to Lori.

But he couldn't bring up Lori's face.

All he could see was Peyton's.

He buried his face in his hands as guilt the size of the Alamo weighed him down. What had happened to his good judgment? His control?

Control was impossible around Peyton. He'd known that the first moment she'd scorched him with those blue eyes.

He stood and reached for his clothes. He had to talk to her.

Thank God she'd gone back to her room. That could have been a disaster.

As soon as he opened the door, he heard voices coming from the kitchen.

"What are we having this morning, Peyton?" That was Jody.

"How about frozen waffles?" Peyton answered, and a sliver of excitement pierced him. Where was his control?

He took a detour into the bathroom to shave and to get his emotions in order.

"Hurry, Wyatt," his mother called. "Or we're going to miss Sunday school again."

He wiped his face and walked into the kitchen.

"Mornin', Daddy," Jody mumbled, her mouth full of waffle. "We're having waffles with blueberry syrup. Peyton and me found 'em in the freezer section. They're yum-yum good. Want some?"

"Just coffee." He poured a cup and leaned against the cabinet. He didn't look at Peyton.

"Peyton's always finding new things for us to eat and they're good," Mae said, "You need to try one, son. Now I'm going to get dressed. Peyton's singing this morning. Hurry, everybody."

Peyton pushed back her chair and his traitorous eyes zoomed to her flushed cheeks, her shining come-get-me eyes. God, she was a beautiful woman, especially with her hair loose and tumbling around her shoulders.

"Let's go, Jody girl," Peyton said.

Mae stopped in the doorway. Wyatt paused with his cup halfway to his mouth. He waited for his daughter to angrily deny she was a girl, but she smiled, really smiled. He felt a jolt to his heart.

She looked up at him, blueberry syrup on her chin. "Daddy, can I have some shorts like Peyton's?"

"Sure." He reached for a napkin and wiped away the syrup.

"And some sandals with pretty rhinestones on them?"

"Okay."

"Good. Peyton'll help me pick some out." She ran for the hall, Dolittle sprinting after her.

"My, my," Mae said. "Isn't that something?"

"Yes, it is." His eyes locked with Peyton's and she winked. Any control he had went south, where all his emotions seemed to be centered.

THEY MADE IT to Sunday school on time and then everyone filed into the small church for Pastor Johnson's sermon. Peyton heard very little. She was concentrating on her solo performance. The pastor had asked her to sing "The Old Rugged Cross" again and she'd chosen to follow it with "Amazing Grace."

She was nervous, but dressed for the occasion. Miss Hattie's Tea Room had a small gift shop that sold a little bit of everything. One day after she and Angie had lunch, Peyton found a sleeveless V-neck black dress that came to just below her knees. White-and-black beads edged the V, and Peyton accessorized the dress with a white belt. It was her church dress. Her party dress she left at home.

"Now Ms. Ross is going to sing for us." The pastor's voice penetrated her anxious brain. He took his seat to the side and Mae cranked up the organ.

Peyton missed her cue and Mae glanced at her. Peyton stared out at all the people of Horseshoe, and her nerves went harum-scarum wild. Who was she to be singing here? She had no training, no experience. Her father had always said she sang well and wished she'd taken lessons, but that was her father talking.

Her eyes met Wyatt's and he nodded. He believed in her. A gust of confidence buoyed her and she broke into song. Her voice filled the church. As the last note died away, there was complete silence. Peyton held her breath. Then everyone stood and clapped.

Afterward, people who had barely spoken to her hugged her. She felt like a queen for a day. How could she learn so much about herself and find happiness in one small town?

THE DAY PASSED quickly and Wyatt stopped fighting and questioning what was happening between him and Peyton. After she sang in church, he knew he was lost. And he didn't want to be found.

And then there was the change in Jody. Almost overnight she'd changed from a subdued child into a bubbly little girl, all thanks to Peyton. He'd never realized how withdrawn Jody was from the world until today; he'd thought it was just a phase.

Now Jody wanted new clothes, feminine clothes, and she didn't want to wait, so she and Peyton spent two hours in his office on his computer, looking at clothes.

"How are you two planning on paying for all this?" he asked, watching as they commandeered his desk.

Peyton held out her hand. "Credit card, please."

Dutifully, he dug for his wallet.

He and Peyton didn't have five minutes alone and he wanted alone time desperately. That surprised him more than anything. This morning he'd awakened with a plan of control. Tonight control had taken a holiday. He had to stop struggling against something that was good.

PEYTON DIDN'T HAVE to think twice about sneaking out of Jody's room. The day had turned out so differently than she'd expected. It had been like a dream and she wasn't going to question why Wyatt wasn't pushing her away. There was hope for them, was all she'd allow herself to think.

Wyatt wasn't in his room, so she moved through the darkened house she knew so well to the back door. She found him sitting on the porch steps. She pushed open the screen door and sat down beside him, hooking her arm through his.

"She asleep?" he asked

"I think so. She was very excited by the new clothes we ordered. She can't wait for them to arrive."

He stroked her arm. "Thank you." He gazed at her, the moonlight reflected in his eyes.

"You're welcome. Your fee is a kiss. I've been wanting you to kiss me all day."

"Me, too." He groaned and caught her lips gladly, eagerly, and for a moment they were lost.

"More?" he whispered against her lips.

"You bet, buster." She giggled.

She eyed the nearby hammock, barely visible in the dark, then took his hand and led him toward it. Pulling her T-shirt over her head, she asked, "Ever make love in a hammock?"

"Peyton." He looked around nervously. "We need to go in. I'm the sheriff…"

She unhooked her bra and he just stared.

"Oh, God, you're beautiful."

Unbuttoning his shirt, she said, "Relax. It's dark and no one knows we're out here. Your reputation is safe."

"You make me crazy. Do you know that?"

"Mmm." She unsnapped his jeans.

With a moan, he kissed her long and hard and soon she forgot where she was. All she felt was Wyatt and his strong arms and muscled body. As the lovemaking became more intense, they tumbled out of the hammock onto the ground.

They both began to laugh but quickly stopped in case anyone heard them. "Are you okay?" he murmured, trailing a line of kisses from her arm to her collarbone and then to her mouth.

For an answer, she wrapped her arms around him and they continued making love.

Later, they dressed and made their way into the house like guilty teenagers. After a long kiss, Peyton went to her room.

ON MONDAY Wyatt had to testify at a murder trial in Temple, so he left early. Peyton had Bible class, and then she and the kids worked on the mural. Sunday was the big unveiling to the church members and the kids were excited. She was, too.

Jody and Matt worked on Jeremiah and they did a wonderful job. She then had them all sign the mural at the bottom.

Jody's clothes arrived and Jody was beside herself with glee. She called her father, and he had to come home to witness a fashion show. Then Peyton and Jody walked to the barbershop to show Virgil and Ramrod her new "look."

"Mercy!" Virgil held a hand to his chest when he saw Jody in the pink shorts with the pink-and-white striped cuff that matched her cotton top. Rhinestone flip-flops completed the outfit. "Who is this divine creature?"

"It's me, Jody. Peyton made my hair look different."

She'd used a curling iron to make fluffy curls.

"Ramrod," Virgil called. "Come see this ravishing young lady."

"I'm busy…" Ramrod stopped when he saw Jody.

"Don't call me a speckled pup," Jody warned.

"Oh, my dear." Ramrod took Jody's hand and kissed her knuckles. "You're as fresh as the dew on the grass."

Jody giggled and clearly enjoyed this new attention. On the way home Jody almost tripped several times as she stared at the sparkly rhinestones on her flip-flops. Peyton hid a smile.

She stopped walking as they reached an old abandoned Victorian home with a huge magnolia tree in the front yard.

She'd seen the house many times, but today it drew her attention. A discolored picket fence lay in overgrown weeds. Windows had been broken out, and the white paint was now a peeling dirty brown. With its large columns and verandas it reminded her of the movie *Gone with the Wind,* of the South and the Civil War. She was familiar with the subject because of her father; he had thoroughly studied the South and offered classes about its impact on future generations.

In her mind's eye she could see a Southern Belle on the upstairs veranda, her hoop skirt billowing around her. She fanned herself as she gazed into the distance, praying for her soldier to return from the war. And then he appeared, riding into the yard on his trusted steed. She raced down the stairs and threw open the door. A man stood there. His dark brown eyes were flecked with green. He smiled and she propelled herself into his waiting arms....

"Ah."

Jody stared up at Peyton. "You're acting weird."

Maybe she was, but it felt right. She smiled. "Let's go home, Jody girl."

That felt right, too.

Her nights were spent in Wyatt's arms. She wouldn't let herself think about when her time here would be up. She and Wyatt didn't talk about it. That was good, because she planned to stay here forever.

Could her fairy tale come true?

WYATT HUNG UP the phone. "Stu!" he called.

Stuart appeared from the back room.

"Mrs. Kriger just called. Fred is missing again and she's worried."

Stu frowned. "He's at the bakery. That's where he always

goes, because she won't let him have sweets at home. You'd think she'd have figured that out by now. I do this about once a month."

"Since he's in his eighties, I'm surprised he can walk that far." Wyatt shook his head. "Just take him home and hurry back, because I want to go over to the church."

Stu hooked his thumbs in his pockets and rocked back on his heels. "You're spending a lot of time with Ms. Peyton."

Before he could reply, the door opened and an attractive woman in a dark suit walked in and looked around.

Stuart slipped past her. "I'll be back as soon as I can."

Instantly Wyatt knew who the woman was—Peyton's mother. She'd finally arrived. The resemblance was striking, the same patrician features and blond hair, except the mother's hung like a bell around her face.

"I'm looking for Sheriff Wyatt Carson," she said in a smooth, sophisticated, no-nonsense voice.

He stood. "I'm Sheriff Carson."

She pulled a letter from her big leather purse and laid it on his desk. He noticed the governor's emblem on the envelope. Good grief, did the Rosses do anything without involving the governor?

"I'm Peyton Ross's mother and I demand you release my daughter immediately."

"She's not in jail."

"Where is she?"

"Doing community service."

"This is ridiculous." She slung the strap of her purse over her shoulder. "I would like to see my daughter, please, and I would like to have her released into my custody."

"Well, Ms. Ross—"

"It's Wingate."

"Ms. Wingate," he said through clenched teeth, "your daughter had the opportunity to walk away weeks ago, but she chose not to. It was her decision."

She tapped the letter with one, long, manicured nail. "I don't think I'm making myself clear."

Wyatt looked down at the letter and back to Ms. Wingate, who was expecting him to fold like a country-bumpkin sheriff. "Ms. Ross has accepted her sentence and I'm here to make sure she serves every minute of it. It's called the law, Ms. Wingate."

She bristled just like Wyatt knew she would. "I would like to see my daughter. Now, please."

Wyatt reached for his hat. "I'll take you to her."

"I have my own car and I intend to take my daughter home with me."

Wyatt resisted the urge to jam his hat on his head. This woman was just like the Peyton he'd met weeks ago, the one who thought the world revolved around her. As he led the way to the church, Wyatt realized he'd crossed a line he'd sworn as a lawman to never cross: he'd become personally involved with a prisoner in his care. He now had to step back and question his motives and his intentions.

As he opened the door to the classroom, childish voices rang out, "'Jeremiah was…'"

In one sweeping glance, Ms. Wingate took in the scene of children carefully applying paint to a wall as they sang. Peyton was on a ladder, adding fluffy white clouds to a blue sky.

"What's going on here?"

"Mother." Peyton immediately came down the ladder. "Time for a snack," she said to the kids. "I'll be right back."

Jody waved at him and he winked at her. His child was happy. But now…

Wyatt and Ms. Wingate followed Peyton outside. Wyatt closed the door.

"What are you doing here?" Peyton asked her mother, wiping her hands on her T-shirt. He looked away from her breasts. He had to look away from a lot of things he'd allowed to happen in the past few days.

Maureen Wingate seemed taken aback. "Did you think I wouldn't come once Quinn told me what had happened?"

"I suppose." Peyton shrugged. "I just assumed I'd be home before you returned from your cruise."

She's planning on leaving.

Maureen eyed her daughter from head to toe. There was paint on her face, arms and legs, even in the blond hair held back with a clip. Her T-shirt, shorts and sneakers were also paint-spattered.

"What's happened to you?"

"What do you mean?" Self-consciously, Peyton tucked loose strands of hair behind her ear.

"You look awful."

Peyton visibly stiffened.

"Get your things," Maureen added in that authoritative voice. "I have an order from the governor that you are to be released immediately." She spared Wyatt a glance. "And this hillbilly sheriff has to honor it."

"Mother, please…"

Something froze inside Wyatt. Peyton didn't defend him, and he felt the pain of that. The line between them became a whole lot wider. She didn't belong in his world, and he certainly didn't belong in hers. He saw that clearly now.

"Get your things. We're leaving," Ms. Wingate stated.

"I'm not leaving," Peyton said.

"Excuse me?"

"I'm not going anywhere until I've paid for my crimes."

"Don't be ridiculous."

"I'm not. I'm very serious."

Maureen moved closer to her daughter. "I know you're impulsive and that you're angry with me."

"I'm not angry anymore," Peyton replied. "You have a right to marry any man you choose. I'm sorry I acted so childishly."

The *oomph* went out of Maureen's power. "Darling, let's go home."

"Mom, please respect my wishes." Peyton voice rose with confidence. "Go back to your husband. I wish you both years of happiness. I really mean that."

Maureen was speechless. Wyatt thought that was probably rare for her.

"For months you've been telling me to be an adult, to grow up. Well, I'm doing that. I'm finding my own way and facing a lot of my faults." She drew in a deep breath. "I'm sorry I skipped out on your wedding."

"Darling, I understand."

"Then go home. I'll be there when I've finished my community service." She looked down at her paint-stained appearance. "I'd hug you, but I'd get paint all over you."

Maureen touched her daughter's cheek. "I love you, darling."

Peyton smiled. "I love you, too. Now I have to go. Paint is drying and kids are waiting." Peyton opened the door, flashed Wyatt a smile and gave him a thumbs-up.

He didn't respond. Whatever they'd shared was over. Really over. It should never have started in the first place. He'd let his emotions rule his head.

His plan now was the same as it had been weeks ago—to get Peyton Ross out of his town.

And out of his heart.

Chapter Nineteen

Peyton knew something was wrong. Different. Very different. Wyatt took over night duty, saying Stuart and Lamar needed a break, but it was much more than that.

Everything had changed after her mother's visit, and she wasn't sure why.

Jody and the other kids kept her busy as they strove to finish the mural before Sunday. Her zest for the project had dimmed and she tried not to let it show. Sunday morning arrived and she still hadn't had a chance to talk to Wyatt. It was clear he was avoiding her.

She'd expected this after their first night together, but not now. Not after she'd given herself to him body and soul.

Wyatt was still on duty as they left for church. He arrived later. The kids were so exited about the mural that she put her personal sadness aside for them. Everyone "oohed" and "aahed" over the painting, and the kids had a surprise for her. They'd titled the work *Peyton's Pride* which had been etched on a plaque and hung at the top of the mural. She almost burst into tears.

Afterward they had cake and punch and everyone visited. Wyatt stayed a safe distance away. Jody went home with Bethann to play, and Wyatt went back to work. Peyton rode home with Mae, who quickly changed clothes to go to a poker game at Gladys's.

"Why don't you come with me?" Mae suggested.

"No, thanks. I think I'll have a quiet afternoon."

After Mae left, she felt truly alone again. She'd had everything and suddenly it was gone and she didn't know why. She grabbed milk and chocolate-chip cookies, intending to stuff herself until there was no room for thoughts of a certain sheriff.

On her fourth cookie, she heard a car and jumped to her feet. Through the window she saw Wyatt get out of his vehicle. He carried papers in his hand. He strode toward the house.

He opened the door, and at the set look on his face, her heart drooped like a bloom deprived of life-giving water. She wasn't even sure she was breathing.

Laying the papers on the table, he said, "You've completed your community-service hours. Judge Fitzwater has signed off on it and you're free to go."

"Just like that." The words burned in her throat.

"Yes." His eyes met hers and not one flicker of emotion showed there. Nothing but dogged determination—determination, it seemed to get rid of her.

"I'm not leaving until you tell me what's changed in the past few days."

He removed his hat and studied it. "I guess I owe you an explanation."

"That would be nice."

"I crossed the line with you and I apologize. I let things go way too far and I regret that. I'm sorry if I hurt you."

"Bull. Now tell me the real reason. I deserve that."

He remained quiet, studying his hat as if it suddenly had flecks of gold.

"It's her, isn't it?"

He looked at her then.

"Who?"

"Lori. All that guilt has finally kicked in."

"This has nothing to do with Lori." His voice rose. "You and I are wrong for each other. Period."

"It felt right to me."

His eyes darkened. "Go home, Peyton. You don't belong here."

She felt the strike to her heart. "And Lori does."

"Lori and I were two of a kind. You and I are different." He waved a hand in the air. "This is all a novelty to you, but it's real to me. It's my life."

"Wyatt," she pleaded. "I don't understand."

One hand gripped his hat until the brim creased. "I'm a hill-billy sheriff and I live in a one-horse town. Can you honestly see yourself living here for the rest of your life?"

"Obviously you can't."

His face remained impassive.

"Wyatt…" She moved closer and he backed away.

"Go back to your life in Austin. That's where you belong."

"Okay." She licked dry lips. "I'll go, but first I have something to say."

He groaned with apparent frustration.

"When I first came here, I called you every name in the book, and one of those was 'hillbilly sheriff'. I really didn't know you, though. I was just spouting off like I always do when someone gets in my face. I was angry, really angry. But you made me feel guilt and shame and I wanted to be a better person. In your eyes. That's never happened to me before. You taught me about responsibility, respect and right from wrong. Our relationship blossomed into something special. At least it did for me."

"But how long will it last?"

"What?" He'd caught her off guard.

"This is a novelty to you now. It's exciting, but for how long?"

As she paused, he added, "What we shared was sex, just sex. I know that's harsh, but it's the truth."

She tucked her hair behind her ear and looked squarely at him. "I think you're scared of everything that happened between us. You're scared to admit what it really is."

"Peyton…"

"It's—"

"Don't say it," he warned, his eyes darker than she'd ever seen them.

She saw the darkness for what it was—fear. But not even that stalled the words in her throat. "Love. I love you."

Without batting an eye, he replied, "It's not love. You only *think* it is."

"Wyatt…" Her voice became low and throaty, like it always did when she was wrapped in his arms.

He looked at her. "I don't love you, Peyton."

Her heart took the second strike, and the blow weakened her resolve.

"Are you still in love with Lori?" she forced herself to ask.

"Yes. I'm sorry."

The third strike and she was out—out of strength, out of hope and damn out of luck. But she'd known from the start that loving Wyatt Carson was a risk, one she'd willingly taken. Now it was time to admit defeat and say goodbye.

She dragged a breath from the bottom of her lungs, knowing she couldn't force him to love her.

But it might take a while to accept that. If ever.

"Okay, I'll go, but not before I say goodbye to Jody and Mae." Giving in was the hardest thing she'd ever had to do. She was used to going after what she wanted and in the end always got it.

Until Wyatt.

The pain was as bad as saying goodbye to her father.

And just as final.

BUBBA BROUGHT her car to the Carson house, gassed up and ready to go. Wyatt hadn't missed a thing.

She hugged Mae until her arms ached. "I'll miss you."

"Me, too. Now you call, you hear?" Mae instructed.

"I will," Peyton promised.

Then she bent and held on to Jody for all she was worth.

"Why do you have to go?" Jody asked, tears in her voice.

"It's time for me to go home," was all she could say.

"Peyton has a family waiting for her." Wyatt spoke up.

"Oh."

She kissed Jody, hugged Dolittle and ran for her car. Wyatt followed.

"I appreciate everything you've done for Jody and I wish you all the best."

She stared at him, not bothering to brush away her tears. "I had the best right here, but you're too pigheaded and scared to see that."

She saw his throat convulse in an effort to swallow. A twinge of hope leaped through her. *Ask me to stay. Say you love me. Take away this pain.*

He didn't.

"When you get back to your world, you'll forget I ever existed. If not, you know where to find me," was all he said.

And that was it.

He thought she was fickle, her feelings temporary. There was nothing she could say that would change his mind.

From the turmoil on his face, she knew he was hurting, too. That was the only thing that saved her and gave her the strength to get into her car.

Time was on her side. Time to prove him wrong.

She headed for the highway and home. She dared not look in her rearview mirror, because she feared home was everything she was leaving behind.

PEYTON WEPT most of the way to Austin and thought how ironic it was that she'd also been crying when she'd *left* Austin two months ago. Then, she'd been so distraught that she'd missed her turnoff and wound up on the outskirts of Horseshoe, Texas.

Where she found more than she ever could have imagined.

Today, however, despite her tears, she found her way to Austin and then took the loop to Hyde Park subdivision, where her father's family had lived for a hundred years. Her father had inherited the large Colonial-style house and her mother had updated it so many times that it looked very stylish and modern.

The yard was beautifully landscaped with blooming crepe myrtles, oleanders and every flower imaginable spilling radiant color around the brilliant green of the Saint Augustine grass. Her mother loved flowers and her father saw that she had her every wish. Towering live and red oaks shaded the lawn.

She pulled into her spot in the garage and waited for that special feeling she felt every time she came home. It didn't come. With a sigh, she collected her bags and headed inside.

Esther, the Mexican housekeeper, was putting dishes into the stainless-steel dishwasher. Ah, a dishwasher. She'd forgotten what it looked like.

"Peyton!" Esther said in surprise. "You're home."

"Yes." Peyton found it hard to smile, but she forced herself. "Is my mother in?"

"She's in the living room with Mr. Wingate, having after-dinner drinks." Esther nervously wiped her hands on her apron. "Can I get you something to eat?"

Peyton knew Esther was expecting a tirade of angry words and trying to avoid them.

She genuinely smiled this time. "No, thanks. I'll just say hi to Mom and Garland, and then I'm off to bed." *To cry until I don't have any tears left.*

Esther looked perplexed. "Are you okay?"

"I'm…" She thought for a minute. "I'll answer that tomorrow." She hugged Esther and went through the dining room to the large living room, with floor-to-ceiling windows that overlooked the backyard and pool.

Her mother and Garland sat close together on a chintz sofa, drinking wine. Two months ago the sight would have filled her with rage. Now she felt shame at that reaction.

Garland was a big, overbearing man with a voice to match. Very different from her frail father. Malcolm Ross was fifteen years older than her mother, and Peyton realized that age difference mattered in later years. Her mother was a social person; her father was not. Looking back, she saw how unhappy her mother had been.

After falling in love, Peyton could see it so clearly. She could also see how she'd hurt her mother by refusing to accept another man in Maureen's life.

Just as Jody had resisted *her* at first. God, she missed that kid already. How was she going to make it through the next few days? Weeks? She didn't even know how she was going to make it through the night.

Without Elvis playing in the background.

Without Wyatt.

"Peyton!" Her mother jumped up, followed by Garland. "Oh, darling, you're home." Her mother engulfed her in a cloud of Chanel No.5, her favorite perfume.

"Yes. I'm home."

Maureen tucked Peyton's hair behind her ears. "Go put on some makeup. That natural look doesn't become you."

"Maureen," Garland said. "That's no way to talk to your daughter. I think she looks beautiful."

Peyton smiled at Garland. "My mother still thinks I'm fourteen years old."

He winked. "I'll work on that."

"I'm still in the room," Maureen said, looping her arm through Garland's.

"Like I could ever forget that." Garland patted Maureen's hand, and Peyton allowed herself to see the love they had for each other.

And it didn't hurt.

"I need to apologize for my childish behavior." She held out her hand, with its chipped nails to Garland. "I wish you both years of happiness."

Garland looked at her hand and then her face. "Now, I'm a hugging type of guy."

She held out her arms. "Hug away."

Arms of steel lifted her off the floor and swung her around. Unable to stop herself, she laughed.

When he set her on her feet, she staggered a moment and then said, "I'll leave you two alone to drink your wine."

"Have a glass with us," Garland suggested.

She picked up her bags from the floor where she'd dropped them. "Maybe another time." Right now she just wanted to be alone. With thoughts of Wyatt.

"Darling, I want you to know I've written up a scathing report about Sheriff Carson and his treatment of you. When the governor returns from his trip, I plan to give him a copy."

Peyton swung around. "Don't you dare! If that report sees the light of day, I'll never, ever speak to you again."

"Darling—"

"Tear it up."

"Okay." Maureen shrugged. "If that's what you want."

"It is." She headed for the stairs. "Besides, you really don't want to treat your future son-in-law that way."

"What!" Maureen gasped. "What did she say?"

"Leave her alone, Maureen. Let her live her own life."

"But—"

"No buts. Come here."

Their voices followed Peyton up the stairs. That was what she planned to do—live her life. Her way.

WYATT SPENT most of his time trying to find ways to answer the question "When is Peyton coming back?" And the question mostly came from his daughter.

He feared Jody would revert to insisting she wasn't a girl, but she didn't. His daughter now had friends, and he spent a lot of time chauffeuring her from one girl's house to the next. Slumber parties were the norm on weekends, and a lot of them were at his house. Between little girls giggling and Elvis at earsplitting volume, he spent a lot of nights in the hammock. Like tonight.

He didn't mind.

It reminded him of Peyton.

But then, it didn't take a lot to remind him of her. He saw her in the bright blue sky, in the seductive moonlight and felt her in the dead of night. She had become a part of him, just like breathing. After Lori's death, he'd sworn he'd never feel that way again, that a woman would never become the center of his universe. It hurt too much when it ended.

And with Peyton it was sure to end. The moment Maureen Wingate had called him a hillbilly sheriff he'd known it. Peyton had used the same words, the same voice, displayed the same attitude. In the years ahead it would divide them. Better to end it now. Later would be too traumatic.

He blew out a harsh breath and wondered why he was trying to rationalize everything. He'd once been a risk taker, living life to the fullest. Lori's death had changed him. Now he was careful, looking for a guarantee. But life didn't come with one. Life came with love and faith.

I love you.

He closed his eyes, blocking out her words, but they seeped their way into his heart, anyway. He wondered what she was doing. Was she out partying? Who was with her?

It didn't matter. Peyton Ross didn't belong in his life.

Then why did it feel like she did?

Chapter Twenty

The days that followed weren't easy for Peyton. But they gave her time to think. She had to admit that Wyatt might be right. Things had happened so fast between them that maybe they needed this time apart to test if what they were feeling was real. Or if it was just hot sex.

Of course, hot sex was terrific, but she was fighting for it all.

She went over her goals for the future. Up till now, she'd never had any and she found that pathetic. She decided she loved kids and wanted to teach. The kids in Horseshoe had shown her that. She signed up for classes to get her teaching certificate.

July faded into August and she was eager to go back to school and do something productive. She didn't wait for the phone to ring, because she knew it wouldn't. She called Jody and Mae, though, and talking to them sustained her.

She'd found an apartment and was eager to move out on her own. Her mother had other ideas.

"There's no need for you to move," Maureen said early one morning, sniffing the air. "Do I smell coffee?"

"Yes. I made a pot. Want a cup?"

"I thought you only drank lattes with caramel and nutmeg and whatever. I didn't know you even knew how to make coffee."

"Oh, Mom. I learned a lot of things in Horseshoe."

"So you keep telling me." Maureen took another whiff of the irresistible aroma. "I think I'll have a cup." After getting the coffee, Maureen sat at the breakfast table. "I need to talk to you."

Peyton sighed. "I'm moving out. No discussion."

"That's what I'm trying to tell you. You don't have to. Garland and I are moving."

That was a surprise. "Why?"

"He's not comfortable living in Malcolm's house, and I see his point." Maureen took a sip of her coffee, eyeing Peyton. "He's bought this lavish house on Lake Austin with a spectacular view, and we'll be spending a lot of time in Dallas at his home, too."

"What about your job?"

"I'm going to start working part-time. Eventually I'll retire."

"Wow." Peyton traced the handle of the china cup with her thumb. "I never thought I'd hear that."

"Me, neither." Maureen flipped back her hair. "But I really love Garland and want to spend as much time with him as possible."

"I understand that." Peyton carried her cup to the sink and washed it.

"What are you doing?"

She glanced over her shoulder at her mother. "Washing my cup."

"Darling, Esther will do it when she arrives. There's no—"

"I don't mind." It made her think of Wyatt and Jody and Mae and—

"Peyton, are you okay? You're not yourself."

Before she could answer, Quinn came through the French doors. "Good morning, ladies," he said, kissing Peyton and then their mother.

"What are you doing here so early?" Peyton asked, and then

she saw the look that passed between mother and son. "Oh, I get it. Mom thought I was going to throw another hissy fit about her moving and she called in reinforcements." Peyton tilted her head. "Sorry. No problem here."

Her mother and Quinn exchanged another look, then Quinn said, "Peyton, you're not yourself."

She placed her hands on her hips, getting angry for the first time. "Well, maybe if being spoiled, impulsive, willful and inconsiderate of others is me, then I don't want to be that person anymore. No—" she held up a finger "—I am not that person anymore. I've grown up and I wish you two would stop thinking something is wrong with me."

Her mother and Quinn just stared at her.

"What did those people do to you?" Quinn finally asked.

"They let me be me with all my faults. I didn't have to be perfect, but I did have to have respect for myself and others. I found out that I can be a useful, productive human being, and it made me feel good about myself. If you think there's something wrong with that, then I'm not the one with the problem."

When they remained silent, she added, "And I am moving out."

Her mother was the first to react. "There's no need for that now. This house belongs to you and Quinn. Your father stated that in his will."

"All this is my childhood, and I need to leave my childhood behind." Peyton waved a hand around the room, hardly believing what she was saying but saying it with all her heart. This wasn't home anymore. She glanced at her brother. "You can have the house."

"Peyton, you don't just give away a house like this." A touch of annoyance edged Quinn's voice.

"Fine, then, you can buy my half, but I would like some of Dad's books from the library."

"Of course, but take some time so you'll be sure. There's no rush."

"I agree with Quinn," her mother said. "There's no rush, but…heavens, I have to get to work. 'Bye, darlings."

Quinn stared at Peyton. "You really have grown up."

She turned in a circle. "The new and improved version."

"Just take life slow and easy and be very sure of what you're doing."

"I've never been more sure of anything in my life, brother dear."

He grinned. "We'll talk about the house again in a few months."

"Whatever."

"I'm really proud of the way you're handling the mom-and-Garland thing."

"Thank you. And thank you for leaving me in Horseshoe, Texas."

"The jury is still out on that one." He kissed her cheek. "When Mom heard, she gave me a tongue-lashing I won't forget anytime soon. A man my age shouldn't hear those kinds of words from his mother."

"Poor baby." She made a pout, knowing Quinn could hold his own with Maureen Ross Wingate. Tongue in cheek, she asked, "How's Deidre?"

A frown inched across his handsome features. "Don't ask."

She laughed as he walked out. She didn't mean to, but some old habits were unbreakable.

IN THE END Peyton stayed in the house because she didn't plan to stay that long. Her goal now was to get her teaching certificate, and the house provided peace and quiet to study.

Giselle called and wanted to go clubbing on Sixth Street. Peyton said no. Her friend called two more times and finally gave up, saying Peyton wasn't fun anymore. In fact, Peyton knew, her fun was picking out school clothes for Jody and mailing them with a note.

It was then that Peyton realized she didn't need the test of time. She knew that what she felt for Wyatt was real—more real than anything she'd ever felt before.

Her days were busy, but her nights were hell. When she closed her eyes, she could feel Wyatt's naked body against hers. She could hear his laugh, his sigh, and she wondered if he missed her at all.

Or if he was just marking time again.

IN A FEW WEEKS a lot of things in Wyatt's life had changed. Or if he was honest, he would admit that Peyton had changed him. They didn't make Sunday visits to the cemetery anymore. He and his mother had talked and agreed to visit only on special occasions. They had to stop grieving.

And again if he was honest, he'd admit that he already had. But honesty might cause him more pain than he was willing to experience.

His days settled into his usual routine, keeping the peace and locking up the bad guys. There wasn't a crazy blond lady making him nuts. He missed her craziness, though. All he had to do was pick up the phone and call her.

He didn't.

Summer gave way to fall and he still couldn't make that call. He thought about her all the time; it was impossible not to. Lori occupied a special place in his heart, but Peyton owned the rest of it.

The rest of him.

Somewhere in October he finally admitted that. Admitted that a man could fall in love more than once, and it didn't make either love less meaningful. One was his past, the other his future.

Just when he thought he was ready to make that call, Peyton's phone calls to Jody stopped. She'd sent clothes for school, and Jody was beside herself with excitement. Every night there was a call, advising his daughter what to wear with what. But the past two weeks had been silent. He hated he'd been right. Peyton was back in her world and she was slowly forgetting about them. About him.

These days he didn't even think about calling. It was over, really over, and he had to find a way to forget Peyton.

But he couldn't seem to do that without snapping at everyone. He curbed his grouchiness as he took a call from Thelma Boggs. Zeke had a girlfriend and was doing well in the home. Zeke didn't even want to go back to his shack. That was the best news he'd heard in a while. His first thought was that he had to tell Peyton. But Peyton wasn't here. Or ever likely to be again.

Loud music disrupted the quiet of his office. What the hell? Stuart came in, frowning.

"What's going on out there?" Wyatt asked, not able to keep the grouchiness at bay.

"Some lady in a Camry is talking to Hardy."

"Tell Hardy to talk to his girlfriends elsewhere and have some respect for other people's privacy."

Stu's eye twitched. "I don't know, Sheriff. He's the D.A. and—"

"Never mind." Wyatt grabbed his hat. "I'll take care of it."

The car was parked in front of the courthouse. The windows were tinted and up. Still, the music was blaring at the sound-barrier level. Hardy was nowhere in sight.

He tapped on the window.

The window slowly went down. His heart did a lung-buster. Sky-blue eyes stared back at him. *Peyton!*

"Hi, Wyatt!" she shouted above the music. "Is something wrong?"

"Turn down the music."

"Oh, sorry." She pushed a button to turn off the CD player.

"What are you doing here?"

She opened the door and got out. He stepped back. Her hair was longer and she wore black slacks, heels and a blue pullover sweater that looked like cashmere. It matched her eyes and she looked gorgeous. Breathtaking.

"I came to see Hardy."

"What?" That threw him and he tried to concentrate on what she was saying, instead of eating her up with his eyes.

"I've been offered a job in Horseshoe and I'm finalizing the paperwork."

"A job? What? Where?"

"I'm filling a teacher vacancy. Mrs. Kriger's daughter-in-law had her baby early, and now I'm going to fill in for her under close supervision by the principal. After that, I've been offered a full-time teaching post. Of course, I have to finish the requirements for my teaching certificate. But I can do that here in Horseshoe and online."

"What? And what does Hardy have to do with this?"

"He's on the school board and arranged it."

"You'll be living and working in Horseshoe? Teaching?"

"Yes."

"Where are you staying?"

"At Mrs. Satterwhite's."

He'd reached his limit with polite conversation. His limit had been maxed out about five minutes ago. He took her hand and led her to his office.

"Are you arresting me?"

"What?" He closed the door and shouted, "Stu, I need some privacy!"

"Yes. Yes. Welcome back, Ms. Peyton." Stuart shuffled out the door.

"Is playing loud music a misdemeanor or a felony? Does the offense require jail time? Community service?"

He stared into her dancing blue eyes and all he wanted to do was kiss her, which is what he did. He folded like a hillbilly sheriff in a one-horse town.

She tasted of caramel, cinnamon and heaven. His kind of heaven. He kissed and kissed her, trying to obliterate some of the loneliness inside him.

"What are you doing here?" he whispered into her mouth.

"Bursting my eardrums waiting for you to notice me, waiting to see if you've missed me."

"Like crazy. And you're crazy. Absolutely crazy and I...I...love you." The words came from the deepest part of him.

She stepped back, her hands on her hips. "Why couldn't you say that in July? Why did you put us through this misery?"

"Because I wanted a guarantee that you would love me forever, that you would love a hillbilly sheriff."

"And now?"

"Now I just want you in my life. In Jody's."

"Well, Sheriff, you're in luck. That's my plan, too."

Needing to touch her, he tried to close the distance between them, but she sidestepped him. "Let's talk about this hillbilly-sheriff thing. Are you ever going to let me forget that?"

"Probably not."

"Well, then—" she shrugged "—I guess I'll just have to ask you to marry up with me."

He grinned, feeling young and alive. That was what she did to him. "Name the date and place."

"What about Lori?"

He didn't hesitate. "She's dead and I'm finally able to admit that. Thanks to you I'm ready to live and love again."

"Oh, Wyatt." She hurled herself at him. "Hold me. Hold me so tight that I never feel lonely again."

He did.

Sometime later, he sat in his chair with Peyton curled up on his lap. Everything was right in his universe. Everything was perfect.

"Do you really have a job here?" He kissed her temple, breathing in her tantalizing scent.

"Yes."

"You're not staying at Ms. Satterwhite's."

"No?" She cocked that .38 Special eyebrow at him.

"No."

After a long kiss, he asked, "You traded the convertible for a Camry?"

"Yes. I needed something more practical, something more me."

"Peyton! Peyton!" Jody's screeches could be heard a block away.

Wyatt frowned. "Jody knows you're here?"

Peyton traced a button on his shirt. "Mae does, but I told her not to tell Jody until after school." She kissed him and ran her tongue over his bottom lip. "I wanted to surprise you."

He caught her tongue and for a moment there was only silence. "I have no control over the women in my life and I'm beginning to like it that way."

"Peyton!" The screech was closer.

"Get ready for Hurricane Jody."

Peyton winked. "I'll meet you in the hammock tonight."

Wyatt smiled and had a feeling he was going to be smiling for the rest of his life.

Epilogue

The next summer…

Every day was made for love.

Laughter. Fun. Excitement. And Peyton—his love, his wife, his everything.

Wyatt strolled from his office to his squad car with a giddy-up in his step and a perpetual smile on his face. Slipping into his car, he reached for his sunglasses and headed for home.

And Peyton.

He never dreamed he could love another woman as much as he loved Peyton. Sometimes he didn't understand it and sometimes it frightened him. But he never questioned it again. Or doubted it. She'd brought life to the Carson family and he'd love her forever.

Sometimes he thought about Lori and their love and how nothing is ever guaranteed. He understood that he couldn't control fate so he lived in the moment, in the happiness that was now. Peyton had given him the strength to face tomorrow and he embraced it with all his heart. Together they would face the future and whatever it held.

They had bought the old Victorian house that she loved and

were renovating it, so they were still living with his mom. Peyton's car wasn't at home, so he drove to Magnolia Street, which was around the corner. So far, they hadn't been able to talk his mom into living with them, but he knew Peyton would eventually win her over the way she did everyone.

They were married two weeks after her return to Horseshoe. Once they'd made up their minds, they didn't wait. The wedding was held in the church, small and simple. Quinn gave her away and the reception was held in the room with the mural.

A long weekend in Dallas was their honeymoon. When they returned, Jody was miffed because Peyton wasn't sleeping in her room anymore. Peyton handled that beautifully by redoing Jody's room. She had wanted to do the room in pink and white, all frilly and lacy with a canopy bed. But Jody had her own ideas and Peyton indulged her. Jody had picked lavender and mint green as her new colors, and had chosen a white four-poster bed.

Some of the tomboy was still in Jody. She'd hung a bridle and her baseball glove on the bedposts and the horse pictures went back on the wall. The room was now colorful and bright.

The renovations on the old house were a nightmare, but the whole town had pitched in with the wiring and the plumbing, and the place was now taking shape. They planned to be in by Christmas. They were also working on another project—they'd decided to have another child. Peyton wanted the baby to be born around next May while she was off from teaching during the summer. They were giving it their utmost attention.

He pulled up in at the front of the house. The white picket fence was now erect and painted, thanks to Bubba and Stuart. All the screens and windows had been replaced and the whole place had a new paint job, thanks to his tired muscles. Peyton had spent a lot of time on the kitchen, trying to keep a historic feel to it, but a state-of-the-art dishwasher was a must.

Getting out, he saw Peyton, Jody, Dolittle and his mom on the second-floor veranda, putting a second coat of paint on the railing. His party girl was really a homebody.

"Hi, Daddy." Jody waved.

Peyton turned and saw Wyatt. Her heart did a crazy flip-flop like it always did at the sight of him. Carefully, she set the brush down and ran into the bedroom.

"Where you going, Mommy?" Jody called.

That word stopped Peyton in her tracks as it always did. Lori was Mama. Peyton had become Mommy. And it was the most beautiful-sounding word. "To your daddy."

"Love's in the air, Jody girl, and ain't it sweet?" Mae said. "'Love Me Tender.'"

"Grandma, you're weird. But I love you."

Peyton rushed onto the landing and took the stairs two at a time. Reaching the foyer, she yanked opened the door and there he was—the man whose dark eyes were flecked with green. Her hero, her lover, her ten-pin husband.

She launched herself into his waiting arms, laughing with happiness.

Fairy tales did come true.

For her, it was the day she was arrested—by the sheriff of Horseshoe, Texas.

* * * * *

*Celebrate 60 years of pure reading
pleasure with Harlequin®!
Silhouette® Romantic Suspense is celebrating
with the glamour-filled, adrenaline-charged series*
LOVE IN 60 SECONDS
*starting in April 2009.
Six stories that promise to bring the glitz of Las Vegas,
the danger of revenge, the mystery of a missing diamond,
family scandals and ripped-from-the-headlines intrigue. Get
your heart racing as love happens in sixty seconds!*

Enjoy a sneak peek of
USA TODAY *bestselling author Marie Ferrarella's*
THE HEIRESS'S 2-WEEK AFFAIR.
*Available April 2009
from Silhouette® Romantic Suspense.*

Eight years ago Matt Shaffer had vanished out of Natalie Rothchild's life, leaving behind a one-line note tucked under a pillow that had grown cold: *I'm sorry, but this just isn't going to work.*

That was it. No explanation, no real indication of remorse. The note had been as clinical and compassionless as an eviction notice, which, in effect, it had been, Natalie thought as she navigated through the morning traffic. Matt had written the note to evict her from his life.

She'd spent the next two weeks crying, breaking down without warning as she walked down the street, or as she sat staring at a meal she couldn't bring herself to eat.

Candace, she remembered with a bittersweet pang, had tried to get her to go clubbing in order to get her to forget about Matt.

She'd turned her twin down, but she did get her act together. If Matt didn't think enough of their relationship to try to contact her, to try to make her understand why he'd changed so radically from lover to stranger, then to hell with him. He was dead to her, she resolved. And he'd remained that way.

Until twenty minutes ago.

The adrenaline in her veins kept mounting.

Natalie focused on her driving. Vegas in the daylight wasn't nearly as alluring, as magical and glitzy as it was after dark. Like an aging woman best seen in soft lighting, Vegas's imperfections were all visible in the daylight. Natalie supposed that was why people like her sister didn't like to get up until noon. They lived for the night.

Except that Candace could no longer do that.

The thought brought a fresh, sharp ache with it.

"Damn it, Candy, what a waste," Natalie murmured under her breath.

She pulled up before the Janus casino. One of the three valets currently on duty came to life and made a beeline for her vehicle.

"Welcome to the Janus," the young attendant said cheerfully as he opened her door with a flourish.

"We'll see," she replied solemnly.

As he pulled away with her car, Natalie looked up at the casino's logo. Janus was the Roman god with two faces, one pointed toward the past, the other facing the future. It struck her as rather ironic, given what she was doing here, seeking out someone from her past in order to get answers so that the future could be settled.

The moment she entered the casino, the Vegas phenomena took hold. It was like stepping into a world where time did not matter or even make an appearance. There was only a sense of "now."

Because in Natalie's experience she'd discovered that bartenders knew the inner workings of any establishment they worked for better than anyone else, she made her way to the first bar she saw within the casino.

The bartender in attendance was a gregarious man in his early forties. He had a quick, sexy smile, which was probably one of the main reasons he'd been hired. His name tag identified him as Kevin.

Moving to her end of the bar, Kevin asked, "What'll it be, pretty lady?"

"Information." She saw a dubious look cross his brow. To counter that, she took out her badge. Granted she wasn't here in an official capacity, but Kevin didn't need to know that. "Were you on duty last night?"

Kevin began to wipe the gleaming black surface of the bar. "You mean, during the gala?"

"Yes."

The smile gracing his lips was a satisfied one. Last night had obviously been profitable for him, she judged. "I caught an extra shift."

She took out Candace's photograph and carefully placed it on the bar. "Did you happen to see this woman there?"

The bartender glanced at the picture. Mild interest turned to recognition. "You mean, Candace Rothchild? Yeah, she was here, loud and brassy as always. But not for long," he added, looking rather disappointed. There was always a circus when Candace was around, Natalie thought. "She and the boss had at it and then he had our head of security escort her out."

She latched on to the first part of his statement. "They argued? About what?"

He shook his head. "Couldn't tell you. Too far away for anything but body language," he confessed.

"And the head of security?" she asked.

"He got her to leave."

She leaned in over the bar. "Tell me about him."

"Don't know much," the bartender admitted. "Just that his name's Matt Shaffer. Boss flew him in from L.A., where he was head of security for Montgomery Enterprises."

There was no avoiding it, she thought darkly. She was going to have to talk to Matt. The thought left her cold. "Do you know where I can find him right now?"

Kevin glanced at his watch. "He should be in his office. On the second floor, toward the rear." He gave her the numbers of the rooms where the monitors that kept watch over the casino guests as they tried their luck against the house were located.

Taking out a twenty, she placed it on the bar. "Thanks for your help."

Kevin slipped the bill into his vest pocket. "Anytime, lovely lady," he called after her. "Anytime."

She debated going up the stairs, then decided on the elevator. The car that took her up to the second floor was empty. Natalie stepped out of the elevator, looked around to get her bearings and then walked toward the rear of the floor.

"Into the Valley of Death rode the six hundred," she silently recited, digging deep for a line from a poem by Tennyson. Wrapping her hand around a brass handle, she opened one of the glass doors and walked in.

The woman whose desk was closest to the door looked up. "You can't come in here. This is a restricted area."

Natalie already had her ID in her hand and held it up. "I'm looking for Matt Shaffer," she told the woman.

God, even saying his name made her mouth go dry. She was supposed to be over him, to have moved on with her life. What happened?

The woman began to answer her. "He's—"

"Right here."

The deep voice came from behind her. Natalie felt every single nerve ending go on tactical alert at the same moment that all the hairs at the back of her neck stood up. Eight years had passed, but she would have recognized his voice anywhere.

* * * * *

Why did Matt Shaffer leave
heiress-turned-cop Natalie Rothchild?
What does he know about the death
of Natalie's twin sister?
Come and meet these two reunited lovers and learn
the secrets of the Rothchild family in
THE HEIRESS'S 2-WEEK AFFAIR
by USA TODAY *bestselling author*
Marie Ferrarella.
The first book in Silhouette® Romantic Suspense's
wildly romantic new continuity,
LOVE IN 60 SECONDS!
Available April 2009.

You're invited to join our Tell Harlequin Reader Panel!

By joining our new reader panel you will:

- Receive Harlequin® books—they are FREE and yours to keep with no obligation to purchase anything!
- Participate in fun online surveys
- Exchange opinions and ideas with women just like you
- Have a say in our new book ideas and help us publish the best in women's fiction

In addition, you will have a chance to win great prizes and receive special gifts! See Web site for details. Some conditions apply. Space is limited.

To join, visit us at
www.TellHarlequin.com.

REQUEST YOUR FREE BOOKS!

2 FREE NOVELS PLUS 2
FREE GIFTS!

Love, Home & Happiness!

YES! Please send me 2 FREE Harlequin® American Romance® novels and my 2 FREE gifts (gifts are worth about $10). After receiving them, if I don't wish to receive any more books, I can return the shipping statement marked "cancel." If I don't cancel, I will receive 4 brand-new novels every month and be billed just $4.24 per book in the U.S. or $4.99 per book in Canada. That's a savings of close to 15% off the cover price! It's quite a bargain! Shipping and handling is just 25¢ per book, along with any applicable taxes.* I understand that accepting the 2 free books and gifts places me under no obligation to buy anything. I can always return a shipment and cancel at any time. Even if I never buy another book from Harlequin, the two free books and gifts are mine to keep forever.

154 HDN EEZK 354 HDN EEZV

Name	(PLEASE PRINT)
Address	Apt. #
City	State/Prov.	Zip/Postal Code

Signature (if under 18, a parent or guardian must sign)

Mail to the Harlequin Reader Service:
IN U.S.A.: P.O. Box 1867, Buffalo, NY 14240-1867
IN CANADA: P.O. Box 609, Fort Erie, Ontario L2A 5X3

Not valid to current subscribers of Harlequin® American Romance® books.

Want to try two free books from another line?
Call 1-800-873-8635 or visit www.morefreebooks.com.

* Terms and prices subject to change without notice. N.Y. residents add applicable sales tax. Canadian residents will be charged applicable provincial taxes and GST. Offer not valid in Quebec. This offer is limited to one order per household. All orders subject to approval. Credit or debit balances in a customer's account(s) may be offset by any other outstanding balance owed by or to the customer. Please allow 4 to 6 weeks for delivery. Offer available while quantities last.

Your Privacy: Harlequin is committed to protecting your privacy. Our Privacy Policy is available online at www.eHarlequin.com or upon request from the Reader Service. From time to time we make our lists of customers available to reputable third parties who may have a product or service of interest to you. If you would prefer we not share your name and address, please check here. ☐

HAR08R2

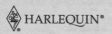

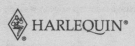 HARLEQUIN®

 *American* ★ *Romance*®

COMING NEXT MONTH
Available April 14, 2009

#1253 A COWBOY'S PROMISE by Marin Thomas
Men Made in America
Keeping her Idaho horse farm going has been a struggle for Amy Olsen. Then ex-rodeo rider Matt Cartwright shows up to collect on a debt. But once he meets the widow and her two young daughters, Matt's the one who wants to make good. And when he finds himself falling for Amy, making good is one promise he intends to keep!

#1254 FOUND: ONE BABY by Cathy Gillen Thacker
Made in Texas
From the moment she comes to the rescue of an abandoned infant on her neighbor's porch, Michelle Anderson is smitten. But when the sexy doctor next door, Thad Garner, proposes they join together to adopt the baby, Michelle refuses to marry without love. So Thad must prove to her that "love, marriage, baby" can work out—even if you do it in the wrong order!

#1255 MISTLETOE CINDERELLA by Tanya Michaels
4 Seasons in Mistletoe
When Dylan Echols mistakes her for the most popular girl in high school at their ten-year reunion, Chloe Malcolm seizes the Cinderella moment. The small-town computer programmer has had a crush on the former big-league pitcher since forever. But what happens once the clock strikes twelve? Will she turn back into her tongue-tied former self? Or have a happily-ever-after with the prince of her dreams?

#1256 THE GOOD FATHER by Kara Lennox
Second Sons
The last thing Max Remington wants is to get involved with Jane Selwyn. Not only does she work for him, but she's a single mom! It's not that he doesn't like kids, but they complicate things. And his top priority is building his advertising agency. Too bad his heart won't listen to his head....

www.eHarlequin.com